WOLF MATE

M GUIDA

Created with Vellum

1

I picked up the crumpled letter that my uncle, King Calvin, had sent to Highburn Fortress, my friend Prince Ashton's home, where I had been offered shelter and protection, and re-read it for the millionth time.

My dear Salem,

You have done me a great injustice by stealing one of my demon wolves, kidnapping my daughter, and freeing prisoners that are enemies of my crown. You have also turned my allies, specifically the Tundra Kingdom, against me.

These are insults I cannot abide. Therefore, I must teach you a lesson.

First, you will bring the demon wolf with you to Iredale Palace, and turn her over to Velkan.

Second, you will then face me alone in Iredale Palace's arena. We will fight to the death.

If you fail to bring the demon wolf, or come with anyone else, I will execute the Vindicators one at a time, starting with your mate, Mateo.

We will meet on the Winter Solstice. Do not disappoint me.

K*ing Calvin*

So. There it was. My uncle had drawn the lines and had dared me to step over them.

My eyes blurred, and a lump formed in my throat. Just thinking of losing Mateo tore out my heart. I couldn't lose him, I just couldn't. He was my mate, and I had never told him I loved him. I wasn't going to let him die. I'd find a way to rescue him.

To do that, I had to beat Calvin. According to his daughter Gloria, who was now on our side, Calvin had never lost a fight. Maybe so, but I would die trying.

It wasn't just Mateo I had to rescue. It was also the rest of the Vindicators: Gunnar, king of the Dark Demons, my Aunt Remi, and the vampire Quint. They were my family, and once again, Calvin was threatening to kill my family. No way was I going to let him. If he wanted to fight to the death, then bring it on, douchebag.

I glanced down at Luna, the demon wolf my uncle wanted back, twice as big as any wolf except for mine. She was lying on the hardwood floor, resting her head on her paws. Ever since I had freed her from the Unseelie spell binding her to the demon Velkan, she hadn't left my side.

"I shouldn't have eaten so much at breakfast, girl." The rich food of croissants, Eggs Benedict, and biscuits and gravy rolled around inside my tummy like a bowling ball.

She whined and licked my hand, as if she understood.

"I'm okay." I cupped her soft cheeks with my palms. "You're

such a good girl." She wagged her tail and then hurried over toward the bedroom door, telling me it was time to leave.

"Not yet, girl. I have to finish packing."

She dropped her head and flopped in front of me, lying on her belly, resting her head on her paws again. I swear she was pouting.

"I won't take too long. I promise." I unzipped my backpack that was on my four-poster king-sized bed. I couldn't help but run my fingers across the soft white quilt, wishing I could take it and the bed with me. No such luck. Sleeping on the hard frozen ground was in my future.

Someone knocked on the door. "Salem, may I come in?" I recognized the regal voice and smiled. I thought she had already left and returned to her kingdom.

I quickly wiped my tears off and cleared my throat. "Sure."

The Fae Queen Gwendoline of the Starlight Kingdom entered. Her yellow gown shimmered as she entered, and a crown of white roses rested on her head. Concern flickered in her lovely green eyes. "Do you know much about witches?"

"Just what everyone has told me." I opened a drawer in the hand-carved cherry wood dresser that matched the bed and the nightstand. I pulled out a pair of jeans and a purple sweatshirt and placed them carefully on top of the Book of Goody spell book that was already in my backpack. That was something else my uncle desperately wanted that I would never let him have. I glanced over my shoulder. "Why? What are you doing here, anyway? I thought you had left for your kingdom."

"I started out, but my scouts reported some disturbing news to me, so I returned here. What do you know about a witch's familiar?" The tone in her voice didn't bode well.

I frowned and turned around to face her. "Um, not much. Why?"

"My scouts have learned that King Calvin has discovered an ancient spell that can turn a familiar into a human. Not for long. Usually, they only remain in human form for twenty-four hours."

I had never heard of such a thing, but then again, my knowledge of the supernatural was somewhat limited. "Seriously? So, familiars are some kind of shifter?"

She shook her head. "No. They are animals. Calvin is sending his special forces to hunt down Hayley's familiar, Freedom."

"Great." I threw up my arms. "Fucking great. The Winter Solstice is less than a month away and it's a race between us and them. What does my uncle want with Freedom, anyway?"

The queen stroked Luna's soft fur. "From what my scouts have learned, Freedom may or may not have been present when your uncle murdered your father, and Calvin wants to find out what he knows about it. Also, if he really does know where the key to the Rose Box is located."

I stilled, and the blood drained from my face. "What?" I clenched and unclenched my fists. "Freedom just watched my father choke on the poison?" My wolf pushed against me. I bared my teeth. "He just sat and watched and *did nothing*?" I couldn't keep the fury out of my voice. I'd rip his feathers out one by one when I caught him.

"Easy, girl. Calm down." She gripped my shoulders gently. "He was locked in a cage. What would you have liked him to do?"

I took several deep breaths and then, when I was in better control of my anger. I gave her a small smile. "How did Freedom get out of the cage?"

The queen dropped her arms, and her brows furrowed. "I'm not quite sure, but Hayley somehow freed him. Witches are connected to their familiars—they're almost part of them. I'm guessing she'd rather sacrifice herself than watch Freedom suffer."

I scrubbed my face with my hand. "God, my uncle really is a bastard, isn't he?"

"He's determined to keep his crown and will do anything—and I mean anything—to keep it. Even make deals with the devil himself."

The bowling ball rolling around in my gut rammed into my ribs hard. "You mean like the Unseelie?"

"And Demons."

"Including Velkan?"

"Yes. If Calvin finds the key and opens the Rose Box, all demon wolves will align with him. He'll be invincible."

I rubbed my forehead. "Well, that sucks."

Sadness flickered in the queen's eyes. "I'm afraid there's more."

Panic flared through me and I blurted, "He didn't kill Mateo, did he?"

"No, my dear. As far as I know, he's alive. But rumors have been flying around for months that there's a plot to remove Gunnar from his crown. According to my scouts, they're all true."

An icy chill crawled down my spine. I paced back and forth. "Oh, my God, this is getting worse and worse." I stopped suddenly. "Does Ebony know?" Ebony had vowed to help me retake my crown and was a friend.

"She's Gunnar's Queen, Salem. I'm sure she does."

I hugged my waist. "God, this is all my fault."

"No, it's not. There's a lot of Dark Demons who would be happy to see something unpleasant happen to Gunnar at Iredale Palace. He's made some decisions that have angered some of the more powerful Dark Demon families, like organizing a Dark Demon Academy."

I snatched my hairbrush and comb off the top of the dresser and then stuffed them in my backpack. "That's stupid. Don't they want their kids to learn?"

The queen sat on the bed and folded her hands in her lap. "Change is hard, Salem. The Dark Demons are afraid that their children will be taught to be ashamed of their heritage and trained to be submissive to the other supernaturals. Ryker had convinced them to fear us and go to war against us."

I jammed my underwear into the bag. "Sounds like Calvin is doing the same thing."

"Perhaps. But Ryker was subtle in manipulating his kingdom. That's not Calvin's way. He's bolder and, I believe, thus even more dangerous. My scouts have learned that he's planning on sending a renegade band of Unseelie and Dark Demons to attack the Hollows to free Gunnar's sister, Kara, and put her on the throne… as long as she swears allegiance to Calvin."

I tossed a small cosmetic bag in my backpack that contained only a tube of toothpaste, toothbrush, mascara, and lip gloss. Doing my makeup wasn't big on my list. "Do you think she'll go for it?"

"She's in prison. The Hollows can be a terrifying place." She flashed me a sad smile. "What would you do to get out?" Her soft voice didn't do anything to calm the anger simmering inside me.

I yanked my red hair back into a loose ponytail. "I wouldn't swear allegiance to a madman." *Especially an asshole that enjoyed killing families.*

"Kara was loyal to her father, Ryker, and he wasn't exactly sane," she said dryly.

I wiped my sweaty palms on my pants, thinking of the road ahead of me. "Can I ask you a question?"

She looked at me and clasped my shaking hand. "You're worried about whether or not you can defeat your uncle, aren't you?"

I nodded glumly. "Yeah, I am. Gloria said he's never lost a fight. If I lose, everyone I love dies."

She put her palm over mine. "Calvin has never fought anyone who possesses the same power as the first king, though. I believe his winning streak is about to end."

"But what about King Christopher? Calvin's declared war on him because he granted me sanctuary. Is he strong enough to defeat Calvin?"

"I hope so."

I looked down at my boots, and a lump of guilt formed in my throat. "That's not what I wanted to hear." I scanned the guest bedroom where I had been holed up for the last couple of weeks. "If I hadn't come to Highburn Fortress to heal after I escaped from Iredale Palace, King Christopher and his people wouldn't be in danger." My voice cracked.

"Salem, war has been brewing slowly between the different wolf kingdoms for years. You can't keep blaming yourself."

I stared into her wise eyes. "What happens if Calvin finds Freedom and the key before we do? The Solstice is only three weeks away."

She smiled. "Sometimes we just have to have faith."

Faith wasn't a luxury I had. I released her hand and pulled my blue parka out of the closet.

"Here, let me help you." The queen held the coat out while I slipped my arms into the sleeves. She patted me on the back. "Comfy?"

"Yes." I put on some leather gloves. "By the way, what's this spell that Calvin has uncovered?"

"It's the *Curasi Perfio* spell." She held my gaze. "When you find Freedom, use it wisely."

"I will." I zipped up my backpack and then flung it over my shoulder. "I promise."

Luna raced over to the door, wagging her thick, bushy tail. I laughed. "Ready to go, girl?"

She scratched the door with her paw. "Okay, okay."

I opened the door and Luna raced out. She turned and looked between me and the queen eagerly. We followed her down the stairs. My team was waiting for me in the formal dining room. A long, dark wooden table had a white lace tablecloth and unlit candles in sticks. My buddy Hades, the little Catalan dragon, stood next to Ebony who got up from one of the chairs when she saw us. Hades had the head of a lion and the body of a dragon, but his golden scales were soft to the touch.

"Ready to go find Freedom?" Ebony smiled as she stroked Hades' thick mane. Like me, she had pulled her white hair into a ponytail and had a backpack strapped to her. She had on a red parka and blue jeans. Her sword was belted to her hip.

Hades roared as if to say, let's go.

"I'm ready, too." Gloria got up from another chair. I bit back a laugh. She was trying so hard to be like Ebony and me, but her blond hair was curled perfectly and she'd slathered on eyeshadow, mascara, blush, and bright red lipstick. Rather than jeans, she had on black tight yoga pants and a long leather jacket. She looked more ready to go out partying than backpacking through the woods.

Ashton came up alongside her and cast his gaze over her. "You look great."

Gloria blushed and flashed him a shy smile. "Thank you."

Ashton led us out of the kitchen and down a long hallway that had fancy light fixtures overhead. "My dad is busy in a meeting, and he apologizes for not seeing us off. The Queen's scouts have reported that Calvin's sent a garrison that is approaching our borders. Right now, my father and his advisors are busy coming up with strategies on the best way to defend the Tundra Kingdom."

Guilt drilled through my heart and gut. My shoulders sagged.

This is your fault. This is your fault. This is your fault.

Ashton caught my eye. "Don't blame yourself, Salem. Really. War was inevitable between the wolf kingdoms. Calvin's lust for power has gotten out of control, endangering all of us."

"I just can't help thinking that if King Christopher hadn't given me refuge, none of this would be happening." I bit my lip. "Maybe—"

"There is no maybe, Salem." His eyes darkened. "You've seen it up close—Calvin's an evil bastard, and he won't be satisfied until we're all under his thumb."

I nodded and didn't answer. Calvin had tortured Ashton when

he had him as his prisoner, and I knew in my heart that the same thing was happening to the others even now. The tyranny had to end.

Ashton led us toward the living room. It had a fancy chandelier dangling from the ceiling, and white couches and loveseats so elegant I was always afraid to sit down in case I left a mark. He stretched out his arm. "My SUV's all warmed up and running. We'll drive it to Remi's home."

I thought fondly of Remi's A-frame cabin. It was nestled deep in the woods near the witch's house and I had had my own room with a balcony that looked over the forest. I'd even had a fireplace and a walk-in closet. I'd grown to love that place—but once again, Calvin hunted me down and Remi and I had been forced to flee. I wasn't even sure the place was still standing.

We weren't the only ones in the living room. Three tall blond men were in the marble entryway. They had swords strapped to their hips, and one of them held a bow and had a quiver of arrows on his back. They were unusually handsome—definitely Fae.

But none of them was looking at us. They were focused on Queen Gwendoline, who swept past me.

She clasped one of them by the arm. "Aaron, have you relayed the information you told me to King Christopher?"

The one with the quiver of arrows strapped to his back bent his head. "I have, your Majesty, as you requested. Are you ready to return to the Starlight Kingdom?"

She smiled. "I am." She turned to me and gently kissed me on the brow. "Return to me, Salem. The world is a better place with you in it than out of it."

"I will." At least I hoped I would. Fighting my uncle one-on-one scared the crap out of me. But if I didn't, all would be lost.

2

Ashton led us out of Highburn Fortress. It was midday, and cloudy. I glanced over my shoulder, wondering whether I would ever see the place again. I had grown to love it there, but it seemed with every home that I'd grown to love, from Aunt Remi's mountain home, to Ashton's hidden cabin, and now this, somehow Calvin managed to rip it away from me, making me once again the nomad foster kid that always bounced from home to home. Just once, I'd like to stay in a place I loved without the worry of being forced to move again.

Two muscular guards held machetes. I wouldn't want to meet them in a dark alley. Thank goodness they were on our side.

They smiled as Ashton walked by them. "Good luck, Prince," one of them said.

"Thanks." Ashton opened the door to his black 4Runner that was indeed running. "Keep Highburn Fortress safe, gentlemen."

The guards nodded grimly.

I sighed heavily. The upcoming days would be bloody for all of us.

Queen Gwendoline hopped onto a white stallion prancing in

the snow. She smiled. "Good luck, Vindicators. Remember to trust each other. Calvin doesn't understand love and friendship, and that will be his undoing."

I frowned. "Don't you have a car?"

She crinkled her brow. "No." She patted her stallion's neck. "We prefer to ride horses. Besides, there are no roads to the Starlight Kingdom."

I almost wished I could go with her. Starlight Kingdom sounded like a magical place, and it would be difficult for Calvin to knock down those walls.

Snow was falling and fell onto my eyelashes. "Have a safe journey back."

"We will." The queen grabbed her horse's reins and jammed her heels gently into its flanks. The queen and her men rode their mounts out of the courtyard and over the drawbridge. They were so elegant with the snow swirling around them, looking like something right out of *Lord of the Rings*.

"Come on. Let's load up." Ashton popped open the back of the 4Runner. I sighed and followed the others, tossing my backpack into the vehicle. There was another knapsack next to our packs.

I stared at it curiously. "What's in the extra bag, Ashton?"

He shut the back. "Cook filled it with beef jerky, potatoes, cheese, olive oil, and apples. He even packed some bones for Luna and Hades to gnaw on."

I followed him around the back. "That was thoughtful."

Ashton slid into the driver's seat. Gloria brushed past me and hopped into the front shotgun seat. Ebony and I exchanged glances and chuckled as we climbed into the back. We each took a window seat while Luna and Hades sat in between us. Luna immediately laid her head on my thigh and I petted her head, wishing we didn't have to leave. For a moment, I allowed myself to dream that Mateo and the others had just gone out for a run and would be back soon.

"How far away is Remi's place?" Gloria asked.

Ashton started to pull away from the forest. "About a hundred miles south of here. We should get there in a couple of hours. This baby's got tinted windows, so it will be harder for Calvin's teams to track us."

I hoped he was right, but Calvin always seemed to be one step ahead of us.

I leaned my head against the cool window, thinking of Mateo. I couldn't imagine what Calvin was doing to him and the others. Tears pushed against the back of my eyelids and I blinked repeatedly to chase them away. I'd cried buckets of tears and they weren't going to help me. I had to be strong, for Mateo and for my aunt.

Just thinking of my aunt made my chest tighten. What was happening to her? Calvin would likely be punishing her for whisking me away when I was a baby and hiding me in the human world, upsetting his plans. A tear escaped, and I blinked my eyes furiously, refusing to let another one out. I had to be Wonder Woman, not a damsel in distress.

The roads that led out of the Highburn Fortress hadn't been plowed and it was slow going in the SUV. No way were we going to get there in two hours. The SUV was warm and cozy, making me drowsy. I leaned my head back on the seat, my hand resting on Luna's shoulders....

I was back at Remi's, but for some reason, I was alone. My team was nowhere to be seen. Not even Luna or Hades were with me.

Something was seriously wrong.

Luna would never abandon me, not unless she was captured.

I trudged through the deep snow, heading toward the lake. The wind howled, blowing snow all around me, nearly blinding me. I climbed over fallen logs and brushed away thick branches as I got closer and closer to the witch's house. Cold gripped me and my teeth chattered uncontrollably, but I refused to give up.

Aaaaaooo Aaaaaaooo Aaaaaooo

I froze and looked around wildly. Through the trees, large black shapes darted between the naked aspens and snow-covered pines. My heart pounded harder and harder as fear slipped through my veins, chilling my blood, but I couldn't give up. I had to keep going.

I finally made it through the trees to the lake. Snow had nearly covered the huge boulder that guarded the witch's shielded home. The only way to get into the house was to jump blindly past the boulder toward the embankment. A spell concealed the house and neither supernaturals nor humans could see it, but I could, since I had witch blood flowing in my veins. I had a feeling Freedom was hiding inside the house.

I made my way toward the boulder.

"You're too late, Salem." A sly male voice cut through my heart like a knife.

I whirled around.

The demon Velkan had a bird cage with a bald eagle trapped inside. The cage was too small and the poor thing nearly took up the whole space. Four demon wolves fanned out around him, their red eyes filled with hate. Luna snarled at me, baring her teeth, and my heart sank.

Shit, she'd been enslaved again.

Velkan's shadow completely covered me. The wind blew his long curly black hair to the side, almost covering his handsome face, but I could still see his red eyes and he flashed me a superior smile. "Did you really think you could free Luna? You've failed. And now we have Freedom too. You just sealed your mate's fate."

I covered my mouth. "Please, no. It's not his fault."

"You're right. It's yours, little wolf…and now, it's time for you to pay the price." He laughed a little too hard, the unholy sound giving me chills. "Have I told you my wolves want to play with you?"

"Luna, no."

She growled and stepped toward me, her ears flattened.

"Attack," Velkan commanded in a soft voice.

Luna lunged at me.

I jerked awake, panting, my arms and legs flailing. My cheeks were slick with tears. Luna whined. The SUV swerved onto the side of the road, knocking snow off the branches of a large pine tree.

"Damn it, Salem," Ashton growled.

Ebony clasped my arm. "Salem, it's okay. You were dreaming."

Gloria turned around in her seat, her eyes wide. "What's wrong?"

I touched my sweating forehead. "I'm sorry. I had...I had a nightmare."

Luna nudged my arm with her snout as if to comfort me. Hades put his paw on my shoulder.

"What happened?" Ebony asked.

"Velkan...he was there. He had Freedom crammed in a bird-cage that was far too small for him."

I stroked Luna's fur. "And...and he had enslaved Luna again. And she...she attacked me."

Luna looked up at me and licked my face as if to assure me that would never happen.

I hugged her thick neck. "It's okay, girl." Then I glanced up at Ebony. "He couldn't really do that, could he?"

Ebony frowned and shrugged. "I don't know. Maybe."

Gloria looked between us. "Do you think this means they've captured Freedom?"

"I hope not." My heart was still frantically racing around in my rib cage like Chicken Little.

Ebony clasped my hand. "It's okay."

Ashton glanced in the rearview mirror. "Let's everyone just stay calm. We're all a little on edge."

I looked into his eyes. "I know one thing. They know we're coming."

Ashton sighed. "Yeah, I figured that. The element of surprise isn't on our side. We need to be prepared for anything."

Gloria settled back into her seat. "Ashton, you won't let my father take me again, will you?" Her voice was small and scared. It made me want to hug her.

Ashton clasped her hand. "I promise I won't let anything happen to you."

She nodded, but from where I was sitting, I could see how stiffly she sat in her seat. I had rescued from that disgusting dungeon and I couldn't believe what Calvin had done to his own daughter. She was nothing but a pawn to him. If he recaptured her, when he decided she was of no further use to him, she would disappear like her mother.

I clasped her stiff shoulders and squeezed them gently. "I won't let anything happen to you, Gloria."

She patted my hand. "Thank you. I'm not brave like you are, Salem. My father…he terrifies me."

"I know. If it makes you feel any better, he scares me too," I said. "And you're a warrior, girl. How many times did you defy your father to save us?"

She turned her head and gave me a grateful smile. "Thank you."

I winked. "You're welcome." I sat back in my seat.

Luna rested her head on my thigh.

I stretched my arms and then cleared my throat. "How long was I asleep?"

Ebony glanced at her watch. "About an hour or so."

Ashton looked back at me in his rearview mirror. "We're almost there."

My stomach tightened. It was almost show time. I hoped my dream wasn't a premonition, that Freedom hadn't been caught and that Velkan wouldn't curse Luna again.

I scratched her ears, and she panted as if she were nervous.

I wondered if she could sense something—maybe the other demon wolves?

It had stopped snowing, and I began to recognize the landscape. Ashton slowed down and turned down the narrow road that led to Remi's cabin.

Luna sat up and looked out between the windows repeatedly.

I ran my hand down her back. "You sense something, don't you, girl?"

She sniffed and whined.

Ebony frowned. "What's wrong with her?"

I petted her side. "I don't know, but whatever is upsetting her, it isn't good."

Hades released a low growl, and his hackles stood straight up.

Ebony stroked his fur. "Easy, Hades."

I met her worried gaze. "He senses it too. I think Luna's pack is here."

She looked out the window. "You mean the demon wolves?"

"Yes."

Ashton slowed down the SUV and parked it in front of Remi's cabin—

Or rather, what was left of it.

My heart sank.

The three-story A-frame cabin had collapsed in on itself. Snow fell on the burned wood and twisted metal. The only thing that remained intact was the main fireplace in the living room.

I sighed heavily and wiped another stupid tear off my cheek again.

Ashton turned around. Compassion filled his eyes. "I'm sorry, Salem. I know this must be hard."

I took a deep breath. "What they've done to this place breaks my heart."

Ebony gave me a sympathetic look. "Calvin?"

I unlocked my door. “Who else?” I angrily wiped off another tear. “Let’s do this.”

Ashton spun around in his seat. “Salem, wait.”

But I refused. I was tired of Calvin always ruining my life.

Always killing my family.

I wanted this over.

3

I got out of the SUV with Luna following me. She stood at my side, growling, staring into the woods. Her hackles were standing straight up, and her tail was in between her legs.

Ashton jumped out of the SUV and glared at me. "Will you please wait? You could be ambushed."

"Maybe. But I think it would be hard with Luna guarding me."

He mumbled something underneath his breath, but I couldn't hear what. Ebony, Hades, and Gloria joined us. Gloria's face was pale and her deer-in-the-headlights eyes kept scanning the woods as if at any minute her father would pop out like a ghost.

I wanted to tell her everything would be all right, but it would never wash. She'd know it was a lie.

Ebony shoved her hands into her jacket pockets. "Where to now?"

I pointed to where Luna was growling. "Through there. That's where the witch's house is, and I suspect that Freedom is nearby." I looked at each of them in turn, including Hades and Luna. "Ready? There's no turning back." My gaze landed on Gloria.

She lifted her head up defiantly. "I'm not going to be left in the SUV. I'm part of this team, too."

I headed toward the back of the house. "Before we go, I'd like to see if they found it."

Ebony trailed after me. "Found what?"

Crunch Crunch Crunch Crunch

I glanced over my shoulder. My team followed me as I led them to the training room. Snow covered the stairs, and I smiled. The door was still closed, so maybe the assholes hadn't discovered where Remi stored her weapons. I smiled. "Come on."

"What are we doing?" Ebony asked.

"Getting more weapons." I punched the code on the lockbox.

"Seriously?"

Click.

I turned the lock, but it wouldn't move. I shoved my shoulder as hard as I could into the door again and again. With each pound, the door inched and inched and inched and then, with a final shove the door swung open.

Ashton clicked his lighter and revealed a store of weapons—knives, swords, bows, arrows, and machetes—hanging on the walls.

"Damn," Ebony muttered. "Your aunt was one badass."

"Tell me about it." I wiped my palms on my jeans. "Calvin's got my proper sword. I want to see if there's another one I can use in case we're attacked."

I held out my palm. Nothing happened.

"What are you doing?" Gloria asked.

"Damn it." I dropped my arm. "I was trying to see if there's another match."

"Don't give up, Salem." Ashton patted me on the arm. "Try again."

Luna nudged my leg and Hades bumped the other one encouragingly.

I laughed. "Okay, you two. I'll try again."

I stretched my arm and moved my hand over the weapons, more slowly this time. Tingles brushed over me. Red sparkles flickered around my fingers and then circled a jeweled dagger.

"That is so cool," Gloria murmured. "How did you do that?"

I smiled as I lifted the dagger off the wall. I unzipped my coat and then stuck the dagger into my belt. "To tell you the truth, I don't know, but I think it's because of my witch blood."

Gloria scanned the wall. "Can I have something?"

I lifted my arm. "Help yourself."

"Thank you. My dad never let me have a weapon." She gently picked a silver dagger and examined it. "I'll take this."

I smiled. "Sure." I looked at Ebony and Ashton. "Do you two need anything?"

Ebony patted her sword. "I'm good."

Ashton drew his sword. "Me, too. I think it's time to go look for signs of Freedom before it gets too dark. We can sleep here tonight."

"If we come back this way," I muttered, as I headed toward the stairs.

"That's not encouraging," Gloria said as she followed me out of the basement.

Ashton was the last one out and shut the door. As soon as we were at the top of the stairs, Luna growled and snarled. She edged toward the woods. I froze, and I broke out in a cold sweat.

A pair of red eyes were staring straight at us.

"Shit," I whispered. "It's a demon wolf."

I thought about using the *Morphello Refulsi* spell and breaking the Unseelie's curse, but the wolf was so far away I wasn't even sure it would work. Even worse, the spell would drain me, and I wouldn't be any use to my team. I could put all of us in danger of being captured or tortured.

Suddenly, the pair of eyes disappeared, as if the wolf had turned and run.

I slowly moved toward the dark forest. "We have to follow him."

Ashton grabbed my arm. "Wait, Salem. You don't know where it's going. It could be a trap."

I jerked my arm free. "This is what we're here for, Ashton. We have to go. Now. Before it's too late."

"Yes." He stepped in front of me, blocking my path. "But not run in there blindly. We need a plan, and we need to do this as a team."

I folded my arms and cocked my eyebrow. "Okay, so do you have a plan?"

"I do." He held up two fingers. "We will split up into two teams." He tilted his head. "Gloria and I will be one team. We will take the back way to the witch's house around the lake in case the wolf heads in that direction." He pointed. "You, Ebony, Hades, and Luna will follow the wolf. Hopefully, we can trap the wolf before he or she can meet up with Velkan and the other wolves."

I shrugged. "Works for me."

Ebony stretched out her arms. "Let's go."

Hades and Luna walked in front of us, their hackles up. Ebony unsheathed her sword and I pulled out my dagger. Just then, Hades lifted his head and snarled.

Ebony followed his gaze. "Found something, boy?"

Luna looked in the opposite direction, her tail in between her legs, her ears flattened.

"Ebony, maybe the demon wolves should split up. We need to follow them. You go with Hades and I'll go with Luna."

She frowned. "Do you think that's safe?" Her voice was hushed, as if she was afraid someone would hear.

Dusk was fading, and darkness was creeping into the forest. Soon we wouldn't be able to see our hands in front of our faces. "I don't think we have a choice. Do you?"

Ebony sighed heavily. "I guess not." She patted my back. "But be careful."

"You, too." I stroked the top of Luna's head. "Lead on, girl."

I slowly followed the wolf in the opposite direction of Ebony and Hades. They would be safe. Velkan and his demon wolves would think twice about attacking Ebony with Hades at her side.

It seemed to grow even darker as we made our way through the trees and I thought about shifting, but then how could I say the *Curasi Perfio* spell to Freedom? Plus, if I did get close to the demon wolves, maybe if I had a chance and my team was safe, I could use the *Morphello Refulsi* spell to free another one of them.

Luna led me down the path that led right to the witch's home. I remembered the trees, the fallen logs, even the boulders.

My boots crunched on the frozen snow.

Luna stopped and then raced ahead without me.

"Luna!" I ran after her as fast as I could, but she disappeared into the darkness.

Crapcrapcrapcrapcrap

Panting, I whirled around frantically. Ebony and Hades weren't behind me. I had no idea where Ashton and Gloria were.

I put my palm on my sweating forehead. Shit, Velkan was here. I just knew it. God, was the dream coming true? Was Velkan going to curse Luna all over again?

"To answer your question, I already did."

NoNoNoNoNoNoNo

I turned around to see my worst nightmare had come true. Velkan stood just like he had in my dream. The wind swirled his long, dark. curly hair around his face. Triumph flared in his red eyes. Luna curled her upper lip, revealing her sharp teeth at me, and snarled.

I covered my mouth. "Luna—"

"You've failed, little wolf. Luna is mine again. Mine to control." He stroked her head and my heart nearly broke.

Luna was such a sweetheart. She didn't deserve this.

The same too-small cage with an eagle trapped inside was at

his feet. The eagle's wings pushed at the sides and its head was twisted down at an awkward angle.

I might get captured, but I wasn't going to let Luna suffer one more minute under this bastard's control.

For a minute, I thought I saw fear in Velkan's eyes. Then he pointed. "Luna, attack."

This time, I didn't stand there like an elk staring into the headlights. I bolted toward the lake.

Grrrrr Grrrr Grrrr

Adrenaline surged through me, making my legs move ten times faster than usual. Luna was right behind me, snarling. I could feel her hot breath on the back of my neck. She was going to rip me apart.

I had to save her.

I whirled around and Luna pounced on me, knocking me onto the frozen forest floor. Razor-sharp fear cut into my heart, slicing it in two. She pressed her paws onto my shoulders and I pushed back on her broad chest, but it was like trying to shift a concrete block. My arms shook uncontrollably. I gasped for air, but her weight crushed my lungs. Drool dripped from her powerful jaws, splashing onto my face. Any minute, she was going to tear out my throat.

Not happening.

"Morphello Refulsi," I croaked out.

Tingling sensations swirled around my fingers and seeped into Luna. She yelped and bucked off me, rolling around in the snow.

Tears blurred my vision. Pain crushed my ribs. I rolled over on my side, coughing miserably, and I spit up again and again. Air finally rushed into my lungs, and I wiped my eyes with my arm.

"Luna, kill." Velkan's angry voice thundered through the woods. Snow crunched under his heavy footsteps. A minute more, and he'd be here.

Chills skimmed down my spine, and I shivered. I dragged

myself to my feet. My legs wobbled and I stumbled. Luna whimpered and crawled over to me as if she was hurt.

"Come on, girl. Time to go."

Luna got up on her feet and swayed unsteadily. She was teetering back and forth as badly as I was. We had to get out of here.

Now.

4

Aaaaaooo Aaaaooo Aaaaoooo

The rest of the demon wolves were coming.

Through the trees, I could see the enormous boulder next to the lake. "Come on, Luna. We need to move."

I stumbled and fell hard onto my hands and knees. Pain and anguish slammed into me.

Luna limped over to me as if she was hurting, too. She nuzzled my neck.

"It's okay, girl. I'm not mad at you."

She licked my cheek.

I clawed my way to my feet and placed my palm on a tree trunk to steady myself. "Luna, come. We've got…to get to the…witch's house."

I swayed again as I made my way to the boulder and climbed onto the rocks that led to the top of the rock. "Luna…you have… to jump."

Not sure I would even make it, I drew on every ounce of strength I had inside me and leaped. Cold air rushed over me and the next thing I knew, I was rolling on the hard floor of Hayley's crumpled home.

"Please, Luna, jump."

As if by magic, she burst into the home, her legs flailing in the air like she was trying to fly. She landed with a thud and rolled around, yelping.

I crawled over to her. "You okay, girl?" I ran my palms over her back and legs to make sure nothing was broken.

She licked my hand.

I gave her a hug. "They can't get us here." At least I hoped that was still true.

Weariness overcame me. My arms dropped to my sides as if they had suddenly turned to overcooked spaghetti. I couldn't even hug Luna. My breath turned shallow. This wasn't good. My eyes fluttered shut.

Using the *Morphello Refulsi* spell had completely drained me. If Velkan found me, I'd be helpless. He'd either kill me or drag me back to Iredale Palace. I was totally screwed.

I woke to something wet and soft licking my cheek. I slowly opened my eyes to see Luna looking down at me.

"Hey, girl. I guess we survived."

She tilted her head back and forth and then sat back on her haunches.

"You're right. I guess it's time to get up." I crossed my legs and rolled to a seat. Sunlight was streaming through the cracked windows. The witch Hayley's home was just as I remembered it—ripped and torn furniture, splintered and cracked wooden furniture, and paper and books tossed all over the floor. Yep, it was still a complete mess.

My stomach growled. I knew for sure there wasn't a scrap of food in this place, and I wouldn't trust the water.

That wasn't the only problem. My team would be worried

about me, and I could only hope they were in better shape than Luna and I were.

I forced myself to stand, but I wobbled. Food would help regain my strength, but that wasn't happening anytime soon. Queen Gwendoline had said that witches almost felt that their familiars were part of them. Maybe there was something in this place that would show me where Freedom was. Hopefully, he wasn't the poor eagle trapped in that tiny cage.

The bookcases were in a shambles and didn't have a single book left in them. Shelves were busted and collapsed onto one another. Beaten up books littered the hardwood floor. Bindings were threaded. Loose pages were wet, torn, or scattered on the floor.

I wasn't sure if this was going to work or not, but I held out my shaking palm. "Show me Freedom."

Strange sensations moved through me, making me shiver, but the pink sparkles didn't appear. Maybe I was still too weak.

I dropped my arm. "Damn it."

Then something in the corner caught my eye. It was a broken picture frame, and for some reason, I was drawn to it. I shuffled over and picked up the frame that had a photo of a tall spruce tree on the edge of a cliff that looked over a ravine.

"Oh my God, Luna. I think I found where Freedom may be."

Luna looked at me curiously.

There were no eagles or nests in the photo, but the hair on the back of my neck quivered. I looked closer and gasped. Gold talons were gripping one of the thick branches that hid whatever creature it was. This was it. This had to be Freedom's home. The problem was that this could be anywhere in the Rocky Mountains.

I carefully removed the photograph from the frame and folded it into a square that fit neatly in the back pocket of my jeans. "We need to get back to the others."

I slowly approached the front door and cracked it open. A gray wolf was sniffing along the edge of the lake, and I smiled. It was Ashton. I'd recognize his wolf anywhere.

I patted my thigh. "Come on, Luna. The coast is clear. We're leaving."

Luna trotted over to me and I stroked her head. "Ready, girl? We have to jump again."

Taking a deep breath, I backed up. I bolted across the floor and leapt through the door. I missed the boulder and landed spread eagled on the frozen lake. Cracks splintered underneath me.

Luna whined behind me and paced back and forth, then put a paw on the ice.

Oh shit.

"No, Luna. You'll fall in. Jump, girl. Jump."

"Salem, crawl to me." Ashton had shifted and was motioning desperately with his hands. He was buck naked and looked like a worried Greek god with his defined muscles and glorious golden hair.

I gritted my teeth and slid inch by inch. The embankment seemed like it was miles away.

Crack Crack Crack

The splinters widened and freezing water seeped around me, slowly sneaking into my jacket and jeans, drenching my body. My heart rate jumped higher and higher. My skin turned ice cold. I shivered, but I focused on Ashton, determined to crawl toward him.

Luna's whines had turned frantic. She let out a long, mournful howl.

EEEE-OOOO EEEE-OOOO EEEE-OOOO

Behind, Gloria burst out of the forest.

"Oh, no, Salem." She covered her mouth with her hands.

Ashton bellowed, "Go get Hades. He's the only one that can save her."

"Look!" Gloria pointed. "What is that?"

The ice snapped and my legs fell into the cold water, stealing my breath. I frantically clawed at the ice that swung up like a topsy-turvy frozen paddle board, but my body sank further into the freezing water and I gulped down water. Panic seized me.

I can't breathe. I can't breathe.

I kicked my legs, trying to get back onto the piece of ice. I spit out water.

"Ashton, help…me."

The piece of ice slipped out of my hands and spun out onto the lake. I tried to grab the edge of it, but my hands were frozen and my heavy wet clothes pulled me down.

EEEE-OOOO

Luna's howl sounded pitiful.

"Ashton, please."

He raced to the edge closest to me. "Salem, hang on. Gloria's gone to get Hades. He'll be here soon."

I kicked as hard as I could, but my hands were slipping. "I can't…stay…up." With each word, I spit out water. God, I was going to drown.

All I could think of was Mateo. That I would never see him again. Tears splashed down my cheeks.

Ashton's face paled and his eyes widened. "*Oh, shit.*"

A dark shadow passed over me.

KR-KR-KREEEE KR-KR-KREEE

Luna growled and snarled.

Crap, what was it?

The next thing I knew, something sharp grabbed my shoulders and yanked me out of the water, leaving my arms and legs thrashing frantically. I looked up to see a sea of black feathers. It was an eagle! The biggest damned eagle I had ever seen.

The bird dropped me next to Ashton. I was soaking wet and shivering, and my teeth chattered. He pulled me into his arms. "Salem, dear Salem." He kissed my frozen cheek. "I thought I'd lost you. We have to get you out of those wet clothes before you freeze to death."

My rescuer soared over the trees and away toward a rocky mountain.

Thud

Luna had jumped gracefully onto the embankment. She hurried over to me, nuzzling my neck.

I looked up into frantic blue eyes. "Ash-Ash-Ashton, I th-th-think th-th-that was Fr-Fre-Freedom."

He stroked my wet hair. "I think you're right, but we can't worry about that now. We have to get you out of here."

Suddenly, Hades landed next to me. He touched my nose with his as if to say it's okay, I'm here.

"Hades, take her back to Remi's house as fast as you can." Ashton unwound his arms from me and what little warmth I had felt disappeared.

Cold seized me like a straitjacket, cutting off my air.

Hades swooped down on me and grabbed me up with his paws and mouth. His claws bit into my shoulders and his mouth held onto the back of my jacket. He unfurled his wings again, lunged into the air, and shot over the trees like a bullet, heading toward Remi's burnt-out cabin.

A black bat with huge red eyes that I recognized as Ebony flew toward us. She banked, turned, and Hades followed her.

I looked down through the trees and my heart stopped. A red-eyed wolf stared up at me, tracking us. It wasn't Luna.

Two more wolves joined it and then Velkan came out of a grove of naked aspens like a bad omen. They were trailing us.

"F-f-faster, Hades. F-f-ollowed."

Normally, Hades would have fought them off, but he had his paws and mouth full carrying me. The bat soared around and slammed into a dead tree, toppling it over. Hopefully, that would slow the bastards down. Hades lunged into some dark clouds, trying to lose them. He circled around Remi's home and dropped me off in front.

He jumped back into the air and flew toward our trackers. I

wrapped my arms around my waist, shivering and stumbling toward the stairs. Everything inside me was frozen—my frosted heart could barely thump, and my lungs could only suck in shallow breaths.

I came around to the side of the house and studied the woods, but I didn't see anyone. Not Luna, not Ashton, not Gloria.

Please, let them be all right.

I placed my foot on the first step, and then—

Boom Boom Boom

I fell down the stairs, crashing my soaking wet body against every brutal step. I lay in a crumpled heap at the bottom of the steps. Every inch of me throbbed and every time my heart beat, the pain got worse and worse.

"Salem." Someone raced down the steps.

Ashton picked me up in his arms. "God, girl. You're a mess."

I laid my head against his warm chest. "Th-the others?"

"They're fine. They're right behind me. Hades chased Velkan and the other wolves off."

He punched in the code to open the lockbox and whisked me inside. He immediately set me down on the cold floor. "Listen to me, Salem." He unzipped my coat and tugged my arms free. "You have to shift." He stripped off my sweatshirt.

My teeth chattered so badly I couldn't even talk.

He flicked off my bra. "Your wolf will be able to keep you warm. Otherwise, you're in danger of going into hypothermia or catching pneumonia."

I didn't argue. My wolf was pushing against me. She wanted out, sensing that I was in trouble.

Ashton stripped me out of my jeans. I clutched his arm hard.

He frowned. "What?"

"Back-back-back pock-pock—" I couldn't even get the words out.

"There's something in your back pocket?"

I nodded as I got down on all fours. My wolf didn't hesitate and burst through. My bones and muscles shifted and her warm fur spread over me, taking away some of the chill. I was still freezing.

Ashton searched my pockets. “Is this it?”

I nodded my head.

He studied it. “This is where you think Freedom lives?”

I licked his hand, and he smiled. He touched my nose. “Damn. Your nose is too warm.”

He placed the picture down on the floor and then shifted. His wolf snuggled up to mine and the body warmth spread over me. He was such a good friend, but I couldn’t help but wish that it was Mateo nuzzling next to me.

5

Click Click Click Click

Luna burst into the room and immediately joined us. She wrapped her body around me like a blanket. I rested my head on her thick, furry neck. The warmth of her body together with Ashton's slowly thawed my frozen blood. The ice around my heart and lungs cracked and melted.

Soft footsteps crept down the stairs.

I lifted my head. Gloria stood in the doorway. "Salem…you're okay." She raced over to me and hugged me. "I'm so glad." She released me. "But I need to tell you something. Hades and Ebony have one of the demon wolves cornered. I think he's wounded." She bit her lip. "What do you think we should do?"

Luna whined softly.

My wolf shared her sadness. She wanted me to save this other demon wolf.

I had freed her from the spell. I couldn't let another wolf demon suffer, especially if she was wounded. Where were Velkan and the other two wolves? Was this a trap?

I pulled away from the warmth of Ashton and Luna and reluctantly shifted. My hair was still damp and the freezing cold gripped me again like an icy fist. My teeth chattering and my hands trembling, I unzipped my backpack.

Ashton had shifted back into an Adonis, and he had a scowl that should have turned me into an iceberg if I wasn't one already. "What are you doing? You're barely able to move and you've got bruises all over you."

What did he want me to say? Yes, I hurt everywhere, but I wasn't turning away from this. "I saved Luna, Ashton. Maybe I can break the spell for this other demon wolf, too." I pulled on my underwear and snapped on my bra.

"No, you can't." He grabbed my arms. "The *Morphello Refulsi* leaves you completely drained. What if Velkan and the other two wolves attack while you're trying to save this demon beast? Did you even think about that?"

I gently pushed his arms away. "Ashton, I know you don't understand, but I have to try and save this other wolf."

He folded his arms. "What about Freedom? I thought you wanted to go after him."

I sighed as I pulled on a pair of jeans. "I do. You know I do. I just need to do this first." I wiggled into my thick purple sweatshirt that covered the goosebumps all over my body like a rash.

I pulled the Book of Goody out of my backpack and flipped through the pages slowly. "Show me," I whispered.

The book had always let me know when I came to the right spell before, and I hoped it wouldn't fail me now.

He paced back and forth like a caged animal. "What are you doing now?"

"I need to find a healing spell, Ashton."

Like always, the pages suddenly stopped—*Descenerous.* I scanned the page. Yes. It was a healing spell.

"What, are you insane?"

I looked up at him and sighed. "If I pass out, will you be able to carry me and the wounded wolf?"

Ashton gritted his teeth. "No." He quickly put on his jeans and heavy black sweater, and then pulled on his boots.

"You're not going as a wolf?"

"No." He grabbed his sword and slid it into the baldric. "I have a feeling I'm not going to need it. Besides, as a wolf, I can't carry your ass when…not if…you pass out."

I held up my chin. "Maybe I won't." But my voice was less than convincing.

He grabbed my arm. "Yeah, right." His harsh voice made my spine stiffen, but I didn't argue.

I knew he wasn't lying. My legs wobbled, and a cold chill still blanketed my skin despite my warm sweatshirt.

He motioned with his hand. "Lead on, Gloria."

She hurried up the stairs, not even needing to grab the railing. "It's...it's not far from here."

Ashton escorted me up the stairs, and I didn't protest. My body still throbbed from my last spill down the icy stairwell.

He stole a sideways glance at me. "You're moving a little slow there, Salem."

I shrugged. "That happens when you fall down the stairs."

Gloria waited for us and pointed through the trees. "There. They have him cornered against a boulder and some trees."

Ashton scanned the woods, hunting for anything that shouldn't be out of place.

Luna came up alongside me and looked up at me with big, sad, red eyes.

I petted her soft head. "Don't worry, girl. We'll help your buddy. I promise."

Luna wagged her tail and trotted ahead of us toward the forest where Gloria was already disappearing through the pines.

Ashton grunted. "Come on. Stay close to me."

Each time my boots sank into the deep fluffy white powder, I had to lift my legs high to pull them free and I winced from the throbbing pain. "I'm not going anywhere, Ashton." I didn't want to tell him so, but I was actually glad he was hanging onto me. I'm not sure I could have walked without falling.

Gloria kept moving through the trees and Luna sprinted up to be with her.

Aaaaaooo

She let out a mournful howl and raced ahead of Gloria, who ran after her.

What were they doing? I quickened my step. "Gloria, Luna… No. Wait."

Whomp

Suddenly, Ashton tossed me over his shoulder like a sack of laundry.

I clenched my fists and banged hard on his back. "What are you doing? Put. Me. Down."

He ran ahead. "Keeping you from seriously hurting yourself." His condescending tone only made me slap his back harder.

Every time he moved, I slammed down on his broad shoulder and winced. The air sucked out of my lungs. "Ashton, I mean it. You're hurting me."

Loud snarls echoed through the forest. It had to be Hades.

He stopped. "Oh, *shit*."

Grrrrrr Grrrrr Grrrrr

I tried to see what was happening, but all I saw was Ashton's long blond hair and his shoulder. "What? What? Ashton, let me see."

He gently put me down.

I gasped and put my hand over my mouth. "Oh, no."

Ebony and Hades had trapped a snarling wolf. His ears were flattened, and anger and fear flared in his red eyes. He pulled back his upper lip, revealing his teeth. Blood was running down his back leg, that was lifted off the ground.

Blood was smeared on Hades' lips.

My wolf pushed against me as if she wanted to protect the injured beast. What was up with that?

Ebony looked at me and shrugged. "Looks like Hades and the wolf had a disagreement."

I hobbled toward the wounded wolf.

Ashton grabbed my arm and jerked me toward him. "What the hell do you think you're doing? He'll kill you."

Luna nudged my leg. I couldn't let Luna down. Ignoring Ashton, I held out a shaking arm. "*Morphello Refulsi.*"

Tingling sensations swept down my arm to my hand. I moved my fingers and pink swirls danced between them, then a stream shot out and circled the snarling wolf, lifting him clean off the ground.

He yelped, moving his legs in the air. I slowly lowered my arm and collapsed onto my knees.

Ashton grabbed me. "Damn it, Salem."

The wolf slowly descended to the ground, whimpering. Luna rushed over to him, sniffed, then plopped down next to him. She stared at me with pleading eyes.

I looked up at Ashton. "Take me over to the wolf."

He shook his head vehemently. "No."

Weariness seeped into my bones and I could barely keep my eyes open. "Please, Ashton. Let me help him." My soft voice was trembling.

"It's too dangerous."

"No...he's...he's like Luna now. I can heal his leg...please don't let him suffer."

Ebony stood next to Hades and stroked his mane. "This guy won't let anything happen to Salem."

"Fine. God, I hope I'm not making a mistake." He scooped me up in his arms and carried me over to the yelping wolf.

"Put me down by Luna."

The beast snapped at me, baring his sharp teeth.

Ashton whirled me around and glared at the wolf. "See? He's vicious."

I put my hand on Ashton's chest. His thumping heart was

pumping as frantically as mine. "I know you're worried, but please...I need to touch him."

"No."

"It would be one...more demon wolf on our side." I could barely get the words out.

Don't pass out Don't pass out Don't pass out

I gritted my teeth and shook my head, trying to not give into the weariness threatening to engulf me.

Ashton set me on my feet and wrapped his arm around my waist. He drew his sword. "If he tries to take a bite out of you, it will be the last decision that he'll ever make."

I was tired of arguing with him and only wanted to, no needed to, heal the wounded wolf.

Ashton lowered me to the ground and pointed his sword warningly at the wolf, who growled softly.

I wasn't sure if this was going to work, but I had to try. I took a deep, shaky breath and touched the wolf's back leg. "*Descenerous*."

Eeeeooo

My weak heart thumped faster, and with every beat, a sharp pain cut through it. The familiar tingling sensations shot down my arm. Glowing pink strands floated around my fingers and swirled around the wolf's bleeding hind leg.

The wolf stopped howling, but I didn't know if I healed him, or if he had changed sides. I would have smiled, but it took too much energy. Gray, black, and white colors spun around me and my head slumped onto my chest. I toppled to the right, the white ground rushing up toward me, but someone caught me in their brawny arms and pulled me close.

"Come on. We've got to get back to Remi's," Ashton grumbled. His chest rumbled, and I could hear the lull of his heartbeat.

I shut my eyes, knowing I was safe.

People were talking, but I didn't care. The only thing that mattered was the beat of Ashton's heart. How I wished it was Mateo's. His face flashed in my mind and my heart sank. I missed him so much it physically pained me. What was happening to him? Was he hurt? My uncle was a cruel and sadistic ruler and who knew what evil plans he had for Mateo and the others.

I wanted to rush in and do something, but the spells had drained me.

Sleep, a voice whispered in my mind.

I wasn't sure, but I thought it was coming from the Book of Goody. Something came over me that I couldn't fight, something that was pulling me into a dream world. All my limbs went soft. I leaned my head back into Ashton's arms, and I passed out....

~

Damp, cold air gripped my bones, and I shivered. I was standing in the middle of a dimly lit stairwell. The ceiling dripped with a foul-smelling liquid from above that stained the walls and stairs. Torches flickered, casting shadows on the wall.

Screams driven by pain made my heart clench and my bowels rumble. The sound was all around me, like ghosts begging for relief.

I wanted to get out of here, and somehow, I knew it would be worse if I went up than if I went down.

I slowly made my way down the stairwell, careful not to slip. There wasn't a railing to hold on to, so my pace was slow. At the bottom of the stairwell, there was a heavy metal door. Oh, shit. I recognized that door. Beyond it was Iredale's dungeon. How did I get here?

All I could think of was Mateo. He was here.

I turned the doorknob, and it creaked open.

A horrible stench of human waste made me gag, but I forced myself to go inside. It was even darker in the dungeon than it had been in the stairwell. It took a few minutes for my eyes to adjust, and then a ghostly chill raced down my spine at what I saw. Hopeless souls were locked in cells, looking more dead than alive.

There was a faint glowing orange light ahead that drew me like a moth to a flame.

I walked by the cells and men and women dressed in rags with faces covered with dirt gripped the bars.

Another anguished scream stopped me in my tracks.

"You must hurry," one of the tortured souls whispered. "They'll kill him if you don't hurry."

Then I knew…I recognized…Those screams…They were Mateo's.

I ran down the corridor as fast as I could, but it seemed to get longer and longer. I refused to give up.

Suddenly, I was in a room.

Mateo was chained to a metal pole. His arms were stretched high over his head and his ankles were bound. His black hair was tangled and his feet were bare. He couldn't move. Ugly lashes dripped blood down his back and onto his jeans that hung loosely on his hips.

Velkan had a whip in his hand and raised his arm to strike again.

"No," I cried. "Stop."

VSSSHHH

He slashed him hard.

SHRACCCKKK SHRACCCKK

Mateo gritted his teeth and hissed. Sweat dripped down his temples. He looked at me with eyes filled with misery.

"Salem, run." His cracked lips and faint voice reminded me of a dying man.

Not happening.

I charged Velkan, ready to rip him apart. Then a tall, red-eyed man emerged from the shadows and held out his palm.

Something suddenly slammed into me like an invisible force field.

The man walked around me with a sinister smile on his face. He would have been handsome if evil didn't flare in his eyes. At first I thought he had on a tan shirt, but then the light glistened off his skin, revealing buff, powerful muscles. He had long, thick black hair that flared over his shoulders.

Power emitted from him, making my skin crawl. "Who are you?"

He shrugged. "Demon." He lifted my chin and squeezed it hard. "I'm

Balthazar. You have something of mine. Two somethings, in fact. You will return the demon wolves to me."

I glared. "No."

He flicked his hand. "Then lover boy here dies."

Velkan cracked the whip again and again.

I screamed, but I couldn't break free from Balthazar's grip.

Mateo's legs gave way, and he collapsed.

Balthazar released my chin and then yanked my sleeve up to my elbow. "Just so you know, Salem sweetie, this is no dream. This is real. And so am I."

6

I woke up screaming, thrashing my head back and forth and kicking my legs.

Someone shook me hard. "Salem, you're dreaming. Wake up. Wake up."

I snapped my eyes open to find myself staring into Ashton's worried ones. "Ashton?" My lower lip trembled, and I burst into tears.

Someone else started screaming. Ashton raced over to Ebony, who was thrashing around next to Hades just like I had been.

Ashton shook her, same as he had me. "Ebony, wake up. Wake up."

Ebony's eyes flew open, and she was panting hard. "It's Gunnar…he's…" Tears streamed down her pale cheeks.

Gloria sat next to me and wrapped her arm around me. "Salem, are you okay?"

"No." I gulped down a sob. "Mateo…" I couldn't even tell her what happened. All I could think of was Mateo being tortured. We had to get to Iredale Palace soon before Velkan, Balthazar, and Calvin killed him.

Hot, searing pain made me cry out, and I grabbed my arm.

Ashton frowned and hurried back to me. "What's wrong?"

"I don't know. My arm's burning, like it's on fire."

I rolled up my sleeve and gasped when I saw the three long ugly red scratches.

Ashton gently took my wrist and examined my arm closer. "What happened?"

"I don't know..." My eyes widened. "Wait. In my dream... a demon named Balthazar scratched me."

Ebony pushed her sleeve up her arm. "Look."

She, too, had three long scratches down her forearm.

The air sucked out of my lungs and I could feel the blood drain from my face.

"You saw him too?"

Ebony flashed her gaze over at me. "Who? Balthazar? Yeah, I did. He's a fucking bastard." Her eyes were blazing with anger and her scowl as well as her tone chilled my blood. Dragon horns were on top of her head. Whenever she got pissed, those horns would pop out, and right now, she looked like she wanted to destroy the world.

"What's wrong? Is it your dream?" Gloria asked curiously.

Ebony narrowed her eyes. "Well, duhh!"

Gloria flinched, and her cheeks burned red.

"Don't talk to her like that, Ebony," Ashton growled. "She was just asking you a question."

"No, you don't understand. Gunnar's being tortured." She turned her head away from us. "I saw what they were doing to him..." Her voice cracked. Then she sat in front of me. "Tell me about your dream."

I bit my lip and blinked away my tears. "I didn't see what they did to Gunnar, but..." I cleared my throat. "But I saw what they did to Mateo."

Somehow, I was able to tell them what I had seen without

turning into a blubbering mess, but I was one step away. My heart had been torn to pieces. Mateo was in agony, and there wasn't a damn thing I could do about it.

A tear slid down my cheek and hurriedly brushed it away. The dam was threatening to burst.

Luna and the other wolf slowly approached me. I stared at them. My wolf whispered in my mind—*protect them always*.

I knew she would never let me hand them over to Balthazar.

Gloria petted the second wolf that I had healed. "This is Remus."

I took a quaking breath. "How do you know?"

"He told my wolf."

Remus gently licked the tears from my face.

I placed my hands on his cheeks. "I'm okay, boy."

"Well, I'm not." Ebony's angry voice drew my attention.

Her horns were still out. She glanced at Luna and Remus. "Do you think we should turn them over?"

Luna growled, and Remus hung his head. It was as if they understood.

I met her troubled gaze. "No. I don't. I think we should bust Mateo and Gunnar out of the dungeon."

She threw up her arms. "How? Every time we turn around, we run into huge road blocks."

Ashton joined us on the ground. "Don't you see, Ebony? Balthazar, Velkan, even Calvin...they're all running scared."

She frowned. "Why?"

He clasped my hand and squeezed it. "As Salem masters her powers, another new Queen is rising, and they're scared shitless."

I scoffed. "I don't think Balthazar was scared."

"I agree." Ebony pulled her knees to her chest and rested her chin on them. "He also didn't look like a guy that was accustomed to taking no for an answer."

Gloria was insistent. "Ashton's right. Salem has freed two demon wolves from their spell. We can't give up."

Ebony shrugged. "I don't know."

"Let me ask you this..." Gloria looked at each one of us. "What do you think will happen if we give Luna and Remus back to Velkan? Do you really think Calvin or Velkan or this Balthazar guy are really going to set Mateo, Gunnar, and the others free?"

"No, but I've heard of Balthazar. He's a really powerful demon." Ebony buried her face in her knees. "I can't lose Gunnar. He's my life." She sounded broken and defeated.

I clasped her arm. "You won't. I promise."

She raised her head and rested it on her knees again. Her eyes glistened with tears. "You really think you can beat them?"

"You beat Ryker and Cormac."

She laughed hysterically. "Not by myself, I didn't." Her laughter died away and her eyes turned solemn. "I always had help. They would have squashed me like a bug if it wasn't for the Defenders and the Sentinels."

I winked. "True, but I have the Vindicators."

Ashton patted her arm. "And you're one of us, aren't you?"

She smiled through her tears. "Yeah, I guess I am."

"And we're growing in numbers." Gloria smiled as she petted both Luna's and Remus' head. "We have not one, but two demon wolves on our team now."

I looked at Ebony curiously. "You said you've heard of this Balthazar?"

She chuckled. "Yeah. From my friend, Rusty. He's a reaper."

"Yup, he thinks he's a super badass," Ashton mumbled.

Ebony glared at him. "Well, he is."

She could have knocked me over with a feather. I ran my hand through my hair. "Wait. You have a friend that's a reaper?"

"Reapers are real." She looked at me curiously. "You didn't know that?"

"No. Didn't learn that in high school or in foster care."

"He and his team, the Gargoyles—"

I cocked my eyebrow. “The Gargoyles? Seriously?” I couldn’t help but laugh. “That’s their name?”

She sat up straighter and plopped her knees down. “You wouldn’t want to meet them in a dark alley. They’re a badass reaper team and almost got their asses kicked by Balthazar.”

“But they won…barely.” Ashton piped up.

Ebony threw her arms up in the air. “Yes, but they had help from the Archangels.”

My eyes widened. “You mean like St. Michael the Archangel?”

Ebony sighed and crossed her arms. “Yeah, and he’s one scary dude. Not even Balthazar wants to go up against him.”

That gave me hope. I smiled through my tears. “Well, that sounds like good news. Maybe Michael will be on our side.”

Ebony gave me a sympathetic smile. “Don’t count on it. They’re very big on free will and won’t get involved unless they think it’s serious.”

That sounded completely asinine. “Balthazar getting all the four demon wolves isn’t serious?”

She shrugged. “You’d have to meet them to understand. According to Rusty, they can be a bunch of dicks.”

I looked around nervously, afraid any minute an angel would pop out of the walls and strike her down. “Dicks? I’ve never heard them called that.”

She gave me a you’ve-lived-under-a-rock-all-your-life smile. “Then you might want to talk to Dean and Sam Winchester.” The merriment in her voice made me smile.

Some of the anger in her eyes had faded, and I was glad to see her horns had disappeared.

“Well, if you say so.” I took a deep breath. “It’s time to get a move on, I guess.”

“We need to eat first.” Ashton slapped his gut. “Empty bellies will weaken us. I caught some fish from the lake and cooked it while you two were sleeping.” He brought a pan that had some trout filets—one for each of us, including the demon wolves and Hades. "Eat."

The wolves and Hades devoured their fish as if they were starving.

My stomach growled, and I gladly took one of the fillets. "Ashton, these smell so good. I didn't realize how hungry I was."

Ashton grinned and handed each of us an apple.

I bit into the fish, and it melted in my mouth. None of us spoke as we devoured our food, not knowing when we would feast like this again. The red apple was crunchy and was a nice contrast to the fish.

Ebony studied me. "Do you really think Hayley's familiar is at the top of that mountain?"

I licked my fingers clean. "Yes, I do. He flew that way after he saved my life."

Gloria frowned. "But was that eagle really Freedom?"

"Have you ever seen any eagles save a human before?"

She looked down at her feet, and her blond hair fell in her face. "Well, no."

I clasped her hand. "Neither have I."

She cast me a grateful smile.

"But we have to get there first, before Velkan and the other two demon wolves," I said.

Ashton studied the photograph I had retrieved from Hayley's old house. "Do you think Velkan knows where Freedom's nesting?"

"I do. I was drawn to that place." I looked at Hades. "I bet you could find it, little buddy."

Hades stood up and flapped his wings, as if to say he was ready. Remus pulled back his upper lip and snarled. The two of them wouldn't be friends any time soon.

The little Catalan dragon let out a loud roar and took a menacing step toward him.

I immediately jumped up and stood between them, holding out my palms. "Stop. We can't fight among ourselves. That is what Velkan wants." I gave Remus a hard stare. "Is this what you want, Remus? To return to Velkan?"

The wolf hung his head and whined.

I lowered my arms. "Very well. Hades will scout for us." I tilted my head. "Let's go. Before it's too late."

"Grab everything." Ashton stood, strapped on his backpack, and sheathed his sword. "We will not be coming back here. It's going to take at least a couple of days to journey to the mountain."

I followed his example and flung my backpack over my shoulders. The others did the same. Hades led us out of the basement. I shut the door, and it locked immediately.

Hades spread his wings.

I smiled. "Go find Freedom, little buddy."

Hades nodded and lunged into the air, soaring higher and higher above the forest. I led my team through the trees, trying to keep an eye on Hades, but it was difficult. He kept disappearing between the clouds and the tips of the pines.

Today was cloudy, so the sun was off our backs, but it meant the air was cooler. We could shift into wolves, but we'd have to leave our backpacks behind, and then when we shifted back, we'd be walking around naked in the woods, turning into frozen frosties.

None of us spoke as we maneuvered through the trees. The ground rose higher and higher and the air got cooler and cooler. The rocky mountain face that was almost a sheer cliff was still at least three miles off. I wasn't a rock climber. None of us was. We'd have to circle the cliff and try to find a less treacherous path.

We came to a frozen river, and suddenly Remus and Luna started sniffing the ground, darting back and forth as if they had caught a scent. They lifted their heads and growled.

The hair on the back of my neck stood straight up. Something was definitely wrong. I hurried over to them. "What's wrong? Did you find something?"

They snarled, and their hackles stood straight up. Black and white feathers were scattered on the ground. Blood was splattered all over the rocks that led down the side of the river. There was no sign of an eagle.

Crapcrapcrapcrapcrap

Ashton came up alongside me. "This doesn't look good."

Ebony frowned and put her hands on her hips. "Do you think Velkan and the other two demon wolves found Freedom before we did?"

"I don't know," I said miserably. "It looks like they're capturing as many bald eagles as they can."

"They're desperate." Ashton knelt and examined the blood. "I have a feeling this isn't just from one eagle. They'll kill every last one in their hunt to find Freedom."

I turned to look back determinedly at Gloria, Ebony, and then Ashton. "Not if we rescue him first."

Gloria shoved her hands in her pocket. "How? The bloodstains end here and there's no sign of them."

"With our trackers." I pointed. "Luna and Remus, go. Follow the scent."

Ebony grabbed my arm. "What about Hades?"

I stared into her troubled eyes. "He'll find us, don't worry. We have to go now. If Velkan uses the *Curasi Perfio* spell on Freedom, all will be lost."

A voice echoed in my mind that I recognized as the Book of Goody.

Use the Descenerous spell. It can heal the wounded birds of prey. Velkan has used dark magic to keep the birds from flying away. Set them free. The Illumiicus Honorulus *spell will break his spell. Then the birds, too, will become your allies.*

"I don't know if I can do it," I whispered.

But I had to trust the book.

"Stay here." I raced after my wolves.

"No, Salem. Come back," Ebony cried.

My wolf was pushing to get out. She wanted to fight.

And she would.

But not yet.

7

Remus and Luna followed the icy river. Like Gloria had said, the trail of blood had ended. There was a fallen log over the river that looked treacherous. The wolves hopped up onto it.

Snap Crack

My heart nearly stopped.

It started to break underneath them as they crossed the river. They sniffed on the other side around what looked like human footprints that led to a cave. More black and white feathers littered the entrance to it. A tiny yellow light flickered deep within the cave—Velkan. It had to be.

I thought I heard grunts and cries. Shit, what if it was Mateo?

I gritted my teeth and crossed the log. With each step I took, the log splintered more and more.

Shitshitshitshitshit

Stay cool. But my panicking heart didn't get the message.

KRASH

The log split in two. I wobbled on the piece of wood sinking into the freezing river, braced my legs and held out my arms for balance, and jumped to the other side.

Thud

I landed on my hands and knees, panting. Remus crept ahead and took a step into the cave.

"No."

He turned his large head around, waiting for my orders.

I hurried over to Remus and Luna. "Stay back."

The wolves eased away from the cave as I pressed my back against the cold mountain and edged closer to the opening.

Mateo, be alive. Please. Just be alive.

"No, Salem," Ashton cupped his mouth and called from the other side. "Wait for us. We'll find a way to cross this thing. It could be a trap."

Maybe. But down in the marrow of my bones, I knew it wasn't.

This was my chance to save Mateo. I couldn't wait for them. There wasn't time. I couldn't risk losing him.

Luna and Remus stepped in front of me.

"Remus, Luna, stay here."

Luna nudged my thigh as if protesting.

"No, girl." I knelt and clasped her cheeks. "If you come with me, Velkan could enslave you again. I can't risk that. Promise me you and Remus will stay back."

Confusion filled her red eyes.

"Please. I have to do this alone. I owe it to Mateo."

She sighed heavily. Hopefully, she understood.

I stood and braced my shoulders.

Ashton was running back and forth on the bank frantically. "Salem, no. Wait."

Not a chance. I was supposed to be the next queen, and like Ebony, I didn't sit on the sidelines, waiting for my subjects to fight for me. I had to fight for my chosen mate.

The light flickered ahead of me. I saw more footprints and more black and white feathers strewn on the ground. I hoped Mateo and the poor creatures were still alive inside. Demons weren't known for their patience.

I kept thinking of my dream. I prayed I wasn't going to have to go toe to toe with Balthazar, but I'd do it to save Mateo. He was worth saving. Even if the only thing Balthazar was afraid of was the archangels, I'd fight him to save my mate and my family.

If the archangels refused to help, and I was on my own?

So be it.

I slowly crept down into the cave, keeping my back against the wall. The tension was so thick I could feel it pressing against my ribs harder and harder, stopping my lungs from expanding, making me suck in just quick sips of air. Black spots clouded my vision, and I shook my head, gritting my teeth. I refused to pass out.

SKRAWWW SKRAWWW

"My lord, none of these birds is Freedom."

I froze. I knew that voice. It was Edward. Supposedly, he was on our side. He'd helped me escape from Iredale Palace, but I still wasn't sure I could trust him.

I scanned the cave, desperately searching for Mateo.

My shoulders sagged, and I hung my head. He wasn't here. The screeching wasn't from him. It was from the eagles.

I shoved the disappointment away and crept forward. One of these poor things could be Freedom, and if that was the case, I had to get him out of here. He was the key to rescuing my mate.

The light warmed my cheeks as I crept closer and closer. I sucked in my gut tighter, tighter, tighter, wishing I could melt into the wall.

Edward looked just as I remembered him. He had the same long white hair that was pulled back into a queue...and the same scowl. Did he ever smile? And now he was here helping Velkan hunt for Freedom. Was he still undercover, or had everything he told me been a lie?

He wasn't the only royal guard I recognized. Bill was here, with his short black hair and that same sneer on his face. I still remembered his foul breath on me when he tried to assault me. If Edward hadn't forced him to stop...

Well. That was one point in Edward's favor.

"Shut up," Velkan snarled. "We've almost captured every damn eagle in the kingdom. One of these has to be Freedom."

Bill and the two remaining demon wolves were guarding the eagles. I couldn't help but wonder what the demon wolves' names were. The Unseelie spell concealed their names from us. Why did the spell do that? Was it something about their names that made them powerful?

Edward gestured to about six eagles that were chained to a wall. Some of them were bleeding. Damn Velkan.

"But you've already tried the *Curasi Perfio* spell, my Lord," Edward protested. "None of these eagles has shown the slightest sign that they are the witch's familiar."

Velkan slapped Edward across the face. "Silence."

Edward turned and stared at Velkan in disbelief. Anger flashed in his eyes as blood dripped from his cut lip. He wiped the blood off his mouth with his sleeve.

I slowly inched myself further along. Prickling, icy fear crawled up my back. The light was becoming brighter and would soon give my presence away, but I had to get closer to the eagles. Something told me I was too far away for my spells to work. Maybe it was the Book of Goody, though I didn't hear its voice.

Velkan approached one of the eagles. "One of you is Freedom, I'm certain of it." He rubbed his beard. "Maybe there's another way to get you to drop your glamour." An evil smile spread across his handsome face that promised death and destruction, turning my blood cold. "Watching others suffer has always been an effective tool."

No. I couldn't let that happen. I stepped even closer. One of the demon wolves turned toward me and growled a warning.

Bill and Edward both unsheathed their swords. Just as I suspected, Edward was a liar and a traitor.

Velkan followed the wolf's gaze. "Ah, Salem. How nice of you to join us." He looked behind me. "Where are my two wolves?"

I forced myself to step away and face him. "They are not your wolves anymore. They are free."

He chuckled. "Not for long. I enslaved them once. I can do it again."

"Leave those eagles alone. They're not Freedom."

He put his hands behind his back. "No. I don't think that's true. If it were, you wouldn't be here. Why would you care about a bunch of useless, stupid birds?"

I narrowed my eyes. "Useless and stupid? That's not how I would describe an eagle."

"*Pestieseo*." Velkan whirled around and spread out his arms wide.

SKREEEK

The eagle closest to him screamed. Its wing had been broken and dangled awkwardly at its side. The poor thing cried pitifully.

I lunged forward. "No. Stop."

Velkan approached the next bird. "Then tell me what I want to know."

Do it now, the voice urged in my mind.

I held up my hand.

Bill pointed at me. "My lord, she's going to try and free another one of the demon wolves."

Velkan drew his sword, and with long strides, closed the distance between us. "Stay away from my wolves, bitch."

I reached for my dagger with my other hand. "*Descenerous*."

Tingling sensations pumped through me, and pink streams shot from my palm.

"No." Velkan jumped in front of the eagle, but the streams slid around him and encircled the crying bird. Its wing snapped back into place. I could feel the energy draining from me, but I didn't care.

I wouldn't let Velkan hurt another eagle. In a loud voice, I yelled, "*Illumiicus Honorulus*."

More gushing sensations flew through me, and the same pink streams moved around my fingers.

"You bitch." Velkan's handsome face changed into something truly horrible—his eyes blazed with fire, his nose disappeared, and his skin melted off until his face was just a skull with fiery eyes.

"Oh, God." I staggered back and tripped over my own feet, landing flat on my ass.

He raised his sword high over his head. "God doesn't have anything to do with it."

I crawled backward, trying to get to my feet, but I couldn't tear my gaze away from him. I was dead, dead, dead.

Suddenly, the eagles spread their magnificent wings and flew, knocking Edward and Bill on top of the demon wolves.

Velkan turned. "What the—"

His angry voice was cut off as the eagles slammed into him, knocking him into the wall. That was my cue to get the fuck out of there. I finally managed to scramble to my feet and raced after the eagles. Their wings were so wide they brushed the walls, knocking dirt and bits of rock to the ground. I stumbled, sliding and ripping my jeans, my red hair dangling in my face.

"Get them, you fools." Velkan snarled behind me. "Bring *that bitch* to me." His cruel voice was like sandpaper scraping over my bones.

Heavy footsteps pounded toward me. The demon wolves growled and gnashed their teeth.

Adrenaline shot from my brain, straight to my feet. I was running so fast that it felt like my boots barely touched the ground.

Movemovemovemove

I chanted that word over and over in my mind, trying to sprint faster than I ever had before.

I could hear my pursuers gaining on me.

SKRREEE SKREEE SKREEE

The crying eagles busted out of the cave, leaving me to my fate.

The opening of the cave was so near and at the same time so far. I pumped my arms and legs faster and faster, but using two spells in rapid succession had made me weaker. It was as if I was a skier, wiping out in powder, falling deeper and deeper. Frustrated tears leaked down my cheeks. I didn't want to be dragged back to Iredale Palace, not because I was scared to face my uncle, but because it would mean I had failed Mateo.

A figure stepped into the cave entrance, blocking out the light. I skidded to a stop. Shit, I was trapped.

GWARRR GWARRR

"Hades." I released a pent-up sob and raced toward him.

"It's the fucking Catalan Dragon," Bill cried out—it was more of a yelp than a yell. Definitely the turn-and-run kind of douchebag when the odds were against him.

I stole a glance over my shoulder and even the two demon wolves slowed their advance. Not even they would take on Hades after seeing what he had done to Remus. Hades flung out his wings and flew toward me. He landed behind me, his hackles up, snarling, daring the others to challenge him.

The wolves, Edward, and Bill retreated. They were clearly more afraid of Hades than they were of Velkan.

That was one plus we had on our side.

SKREEEE SKREEE SKREEE

An enormous shadow passed over the entrance of the cave, bigger than any of the eagles who had escaped.

Hades flew back to me and looked at me with triumph in his eyes.

I crinkled my brow, and I couldn't resist a smile. I lowered my voice. "You found him, didn't you, boy?"

Hades wagged his tail excitedly and then trotted back to the cave entrance. I hurried after him, but once again, my pace was about as fast as a turtle in a snowstorm.

SKREEE SKREEE SKREEE

Hades turned his head, his tail twitching. He was keeping an eye on me, making sure my pursuers didn't have some tricks up their sleeves.

I finally caught up with Hades and together we walked out of the cave. My mouth dropped. The biggest eagle, bigger than a condor, towered over the rest of the eagles. All of the birds stared at me curiously.

Now what do I do?

8

My heart pounded fiercely as I stared at the biggest bald eagle I had ever seen. Hades had done it. This has had to be Freedom. He spread his wings, and his wingspan had to be over ten feet across.

The eagle tilted his head and looked at me curiously.

I stepped away from the entrance of the cave with Hades at my side. "Freedom? Hayley sent me. I need to talk to you."

The eagle stared at me, sizing me up. I didn't even know if he could understand me. The only way to find out if this was Freedom was to cast the *Curasi Perfio* spell, but we were too close to the cave and with Velkan still around, it wasn't safe.

A large, red-eyed bat glided over to us and instantly changed into Ebony. Vampires weren't like shifters and didn't tear through their clothes when they shifted.

"Salem, Ashton's practically foaming at the mouth. He's worried out of his mind." Her tone reminded me of one of my foster mom's scolding me for breaking the rules again.

Freedom stretched out his wings fearfully, as if he were about to fly away.

"No, wait." I gestured to Ebony. "She's a friend."

Hades nudged Ebony gently.

I glanced over my shoulder. "We need to get out of here." I rested my hands on top of Remus' and Luna's heads. "Starting with these two. I don't want them to be cursed again."

Luna licked my hand, and I smiled down at her.

"Okay. Come on, Hades. Let's get to work," Ebony said. She immediately changed into a large bat, snatched Luna up by the scruff of the neck, and lifted her into the air.

Luna yelped and struggled.

I cupped my hands over my mouth. "It's okay, Luna. I'll be right there."

Hades stretched out his wings and seized Remus with his sharp talons.

Remus snapped and snarled at the Catalan dragon.

Hades released a menacing growl as he carried Remus across the river. Yep, those two definitely had a long way to go before they stopped wanting to tear each other apart.

"Salem, there you are." I grimaced. Not the evil voice I wanted to hear.

The eagles, including Freedom, all flew away, leaving me alone.

Velkan stormed toward me with a whip held high over his head. "You have spoiled my plans for the last time."

I thought of Mateo and bolted, my arms and legs pumping, desperately searching for another log or rocks that I could use to escape across the river. Then Edward and Bill stepped out from behind a boulder, cutting off my path.

Velkan laughed behind me. "There's nowhere for you to go, little wolf."

Panting, I stopped, not sure what to do. Beads of sweat rolled down my face and back. Crap, I was trapped. I looked at the icy, roaring river, wondering if I had even the smallest chance of crossing it.

Velkan, Edward, and Bill were closing the distance between us. I didn't have a choice. My heart racing, I ran toward the river.

Thick ice covered it, but there was no way it would hold my weight. Wind blew my hair around my sweaty face, and I bent my knees, ready to jump.

A dark shadow fell over me.

SKREEE SKREEE SKRREE

I looked up just as Freedom swooped down on me and grabbed my shoulders, his talons digging into my flesh. I screamed. The majestic bird of prey lifted me off the ground as easily as if I were a squirming mouse. I desperately clung to his legs, terrified he'd drop me to my death.

Velkan raised his fist and shook it wildly. "Damn you, Salem. I'll get you for this."

Freedom flew over the top of trees. My stomach did constant belly flops, as if it was caught in a loop. The higher we flew, the tighter skin-crawling, heart-clenching, lung-collapsing fear gripped me. I was sure any minute he'd drop me, sending me to my death.

My wolf's usual courage had fled, too. She was cowering as bad as I was.

I closed my eyes and gritted my teeth, not wanting to see the ground rush up to greet me.

Freedom glided and rolled side to side. Terrified, I peeked open one eye. Excitement flashed through me when I glimpsed Remi's burnt-out house and Ashton's 4Runner.

"Please, Freedom." I pointed. "Drop me off there."

I immediately winced. Not from one hundred feet up.

But Freedom seemed to understand me and descended to a reasonable height before gently dropping me in front of Ashton's SUV. He himself landed on a branch in a nearby pine tree. I was surprised it could hold his weight.

Ashton came barreling out of the woods like a madman. "Salem." He rushed over and shook me hard. "What were you thinking? You could have been killed."

"Stop shaking me."

He loosened his grip and ran a hand through his blond locks. "How did you escape?"

I gestured with my hand. "Freedom saved me."

The remaining Vindicators came out of the woods, including Hades, Remus, and Luna.

Gloria ran over and hugged. "Salem, you're okay."

"I'm fine." I tilted my head. "Look who Salem found."

She followed my gaze. "He's beautiful." She glanced over at me. "Are you going to use the *Curasi Perfio* spell?"

Ebony strolled out of the woods. "I hate to be a Debbie Downer, but I don't think we're going to be alone much longer."

"Damn it," I muttered under my breath.

I looked up at Freedom. "We need your help, Freedom. I need to talk to you."

Freedom didn't move. I held my breath. All of us stared up at him. It was Freedom's next move. If he flew off, there was nothing we could do. Hades could follow him again, but I doubted even he had the power to drag him back to Remi's.

The great eagle flew down and stood in front of me. He was at least the same size as me. Hopefully, this meant he would allow me to change him into human form.

I raised my shaking arm and held out my palm. "*Curasi Perfio,*" I whispered.

The tingles moved down my arms and swirled around my palm. Pink ribbons of light glided over to Freedom, swooshing and weaving around him until he was completely encased in a cocoon-like cloud. Something twisted and churned inside for several long heartbeats. Then the cloud melted away, revealing a tall, dark-haired man with a sharp, rounded nose. He was very pale and had the same piercing yellow eyes he had as an eagle. A slick pair of black pants hugged his legs.

I lowered my arm. "You're Freedom?"

He nodded.

I wet my lips. "Can you speak?"

"I can. Hurry and ask your question, please." He glared at me. "This form hurts." His tone was sharp and high and strained.

Gloria gasped and moved closer to Ashton. Hades, Remus, and Luna looked at Freedom curiously. I couldn't help but wonder if I used the spell on Hades what kind of dude he'd be. Definitely fierce.

I blurted, "We're looking for the key to the Rose Box. Do you know of it?"

He nodded, smiling, and his yellow eyes glowed. The acknowledgement sent a stream of excitement pulsing through me, making me tremble.

I looked at Ebony, Gloria, and Ashton. This was the moment we'd been waiting for so long.

My heart thundered in anticipation. "Will you please tell me where it is hidden?"

He slowly approached me and I forced myself to stay perfectly still. He bent down and whispered low in my ear.

"You're the key."

I jumped back, and my brows knotted. I must have heard him wrong. "What?"

He leaned closer. "Your blood is the key. Only the chosen one can open the Rose Box. You possess the power of the First King."

My team crowded closer.

Ashton frowned. "What's he talking about?" His tone was angry.

Freedom tilted his head and stared Ashton down. "She's the key. Her blood and her blood alone will open the Rose Box."

Confusion and wonder flickered in Ashton's eyes as he turned from Freedom and stared at me as if I had just become covered in purple polka dots.

He wasn't the only one. All of them stared at me, making me break out in a cold sweat.

I rubbed my slick forehead. "How can this be, Freedom?"

"She pricked your finger when you were a baby and used the

blood to seal the box shut. Everything you need to overthrow Calvin is in the box."

"Do you know where it is?" Ashton asked eagerly.

He shook his head. "No. They're here. I must go."

With those words, he shifted back into the magnificent eagle and soared into the air, flying away from us as fast as he could, as if Satan himself was after him.

Aaaaoooo Aaaaaooo

Something was moving fast in between the trees, trashing branches, making the ground rumble, coming straight for us.

Something big.

Something black.

Something with angry red eyes.

Spider tingling raced down my back, slowly freezing my blood.

Get out of here. It will kill all of you. The voice quivered in my mind.

The Book of Goody was scared. Not good. Not a good sign at all.

Hades growled and took a step toward the forest. Remus and Luna were snarling, their hackles up, poised to attack.

"No." I jumped in front of them. "This is something evil. Something supernatural that could tear all of you apart."

Ashton ripped out his car keys and pressed the key fob. "Get in the SUV. Now." He raced around to the driver's side and Gloria hopped into the passenger side.

Ebony tore open the side door and Hades and the two wolves jumped in. I raced around to my side and opened the door.

Something searing hot slammed into me, piercing through my backpack and my clothes and entering my body with such force it took my breath away. I tumbled into the SUV, landing on my stomach, crying out. Scorching pain pulsed through me, scalding my blood.

"Salem." Ebony grabbed underneath my shoulders and pulled.

One of the demon wolves, or perhaps it was Hades, bit into my coat and pulled me inside.

"Ashton, drive. They're...they're harpies." Gloria's voice shook with fear.

SCREECH SCREEECH SCREEEEEEE

Those horrible shrieks sent something scurrying down my spine to squat in the pit of my stomach. Harpies? I had no idea what a harpy was, and I didn't care. All I could think of was the pain.

Ashton peeled out of there, my legs still dangling haphazardly out the door.

Ebony desperately pulled on me, arching her back, her arms straining.

I clung to her coat as we swerved and my foot bounced off the back tire. My eyes turned wild. "Don't let go."

"I won't. Ashton, I need help. Hades and I can't hold on to her much longer."

Ashton slammed on the brakes and jumped out of the SUV.

"Ashton, no," Gloria screamed.

He stuffed me unceremoniously into the SUV, cramming me up against Hades and Ebony, then slammed the door shut.

Ebony pulled me close to her. The pain in my back was excruciating. Every time I took a breath, I winced.

Something black darted around the SUV just as Ashton hopped back into the front seat.

Something evil.

Something that wanted to kill us.

I glanced out my window and gasped. The most hideous creature I had ever seen pulled on the SUV's door. It had the head of a woman with long black hair set on an eagle's body. Its feathery black wings were plastered to its sides. So, this was a harpy.

Luckily, the door remained locked.

SHREEEK SHRREEK

Anger flared in the harpy's red eyes. She lifted a talon and slammed it into the window, shattering the glass. She stuck her head inside the SUV. I could feel her hot breath on my skin. She grabbed my shoulders, as if she were going to yank me out.

Hades released a loud hiss, and a stream of fire hit her in the face. She screamed and released me.

Crap, why was she pulling on me? And where did she want to take me? Fear fluttered in my chest.

The only answer I could think of was Velkan. The bigger question was, did he or Calvin know that my blood was the key to the Rose Box?

9

Arctic wind blew through the 4Runner as Ashton drove like a manic down the road. The harpies banged into the SUV over and over. Ashton swerved back and forth and then peeled out onto the main road.

The banging stopped.

Ebony turned around in her seat. "They're gone. For now."

I panted. "It...hurts...get it out."

It was more than just pain. Something was slowly sucking out my power. I could feel myself growing weaker and weaker, and I had to be strong. It was the only way I could save Mateo and my family.

"Help me," I whispered.

Anyone. Please. Make it stop. Not even the Book of Goody would answer and my pleas were met with bitter silence. Shit, had the damn arrow or whatever it was hit the Book of Goody too, killing the voice?

Ebony clasped my arm gently. "Lean forward, Salem." Then she gasped. Not a good sign.

She softly put her hands on me. "You've got a dart or something in your back."

The pain was getting worse and worse. I looked over my shoulder and when I twisted my arm, my fingers brushed against something hard with tiny spikes. I pricked my fingers and was met with stabbing pain. My arm fell limply next to me. "Ebony...pull it out."

"It's got barbs on it." Her brow furrowed, and she bit her lip. "I'm afraid if I rip it out, it'll tear you apart even more."

Tears slipped down my cheeks, and I clenched my fists tightly. My wolf was howling in agony. The arrow or whatever it was torturing both of us. "It's burning. Please. Get it out. We have...to go to..." I hissed as more pain slammed into me. "I have...to save Mateo. It's...it's draining me."

My eyes fluttered shut, and I battled to keep them open.

"Salem." Ebony stroked my hair as she cradled my head in her lap. "I'm sorry. I don't think I can."

"I think I've lost those damn things for now, but I don't think we've seen the last of them. She needs a Fae healer," Ashton said firmly.

"We can't drive to the Starlight Kingdom," Gloria said. "You know there are no roads there."

Ashton slapped his hand on the steering wheel. "Damn it."

"Legacy." Ebony said suddenly. "We have to take her to Legacy. Anton will know what to do, and Dr. Greenwood is a great healer."

I wanted to argue—tell them they just needed to rip it out, and I didn't have time to go to Legacy—but my mouth wouldn't move.

Ashton glanced in the rearview mirror. "Don't you think the enemy will guess that's where we're going?"

Ebony shrugged. "Maybe. But do you have a better idea?"

"No," he said reluctantly. "Okay, Legacy it is."

With each bump on the road, my body bounced up and down and I hissed, trying not to cry out too loudly.

"We'll be there soon, Salem." Ebony softly pulled back my hair. "Try to sleep."

That was the last thing I wanted to do. I was afraid if I fell asleep, I would never wake up. I bit my lip and clenched my fists. Every time I thought I was closer to saving Mateo, I fucked it up. Some wolf princess I was. I was just one colossal failure.

He'd been so brave and hadn't shed a single tear, but I couldn't ever stop crying. The heat burning inside me turned my skin hot, and I was sweating. I desperately wanted to rip off my clothes, but if I did, it would be pure agony, agony I didn't think I could endure.

I squeezed my eyes shut.

Think of Mateo Think of Mateo Think of Mateo

My eyes kept falling shut and I'd jerk awake again. But the poison coursing through me was too strong. My breath and heart-beat were both slowing.

Ebony shook my shoulder gently. "Salem, stay with us." But her voice sounded very far away.

Dying wasn't an option. I wanted to defeat my uncle. I wanted to save Mateo and see his handsome face before I left this earth. I wanted to tell him that I loved him...but my mouth refused to move and tears clouded my eyes.

I gave up the fight...

~

"Come back to me, Salem. I can't lose you." Someone kissed my hand, brushing it softly with whiskers. Whiskers that chafed my skin.

My heart leapt. It couldn't be. Mateo was locked away at Iredale Palace. Was he here or was I dreaming? I had to see him.

Wake up Wake up Wake up Wake up

I frowned and moaned. I wanted to open my eyes, but it was as if they were glued shut.

"Dr. Greenwood," a strained voice called out. "I think she's waking up."

That voice. I had to see him. One more time.

Drawing on the last remaining power I had, I thrashed my head back and forth on something soft.

My wolf emerged, and she pushed hard against me, wanting to be released. But something dark pushed her back down, making her whimper.

Someone cradled the back of my head with their hand and lifted it up. "Drink, child. Drink."

I inhaled something fragrant that chased some of the darkness brewing inside me away. Cool liquid went through my parched lips and down my throat. Strength pulsed through me and my wolf sprang into action again.

Someone stroked my hair. "Shift, Salem. Draw on the power of your wolf. She can heal you." The voice was hypnotic, pulling me out of the murky darkness that had filled me with despair.

I hesitated for a moment, then my wolf broke free. My muscles and bones shifted, and I opened my eyes. The weariness engulfing me lost its grip. Panting, I found myself standing on a twin bed with a nightstand next to it. I knew this place. This was the infirmary at Legacy.

I caught my reflection in a mirror. My beautiful white wolf stared back at me, fierce, and even bigger than the demon wolves.

Someone scratched my ear, and I stared up at a smiling Dr. Greenwood. His tired blue eyes flickered with flecks of brown and green, and he gave a sigh of relief. "Welcome to Legacy Academy, Salem. You gave us quite a scare."

Something clicked across the wooden floor, and I stilled. A large black wolf approached my bed. I gasped—Mateo—but my wolf detected a spicy, sexy scent. That wasn't Mateo. His scent was different. More cinnamon.

Something wasn't right. I hopped off the bed and slowly approached the black wolf. He nuzzled me, and I knew without a doubt this wasn't Mateo.

My wolf froze and sniffed. I stepped away from the black wolf.

My ears flattened. Beneath the spicy, sexy scent, there was another one. A foul one. One that reeked of death and decay.

Luna and Remus lifted their heads. They had been sleeping in the corner, but now they pulled back their upper lips, their ears flattened, and they snarled.

Not-Mateo's beautiful brown eyes turned red.

Fear rippled through my fur and stilled my heart. Luna and Remus came on either side of me protectively.

Dr. Greenwood gasped and stepped back. "What is this?" Terror seeped into his voice.

The black wolf snapped at the doctor and would have leaped onto him, ripping him apart, but the demon wolves and I plowed into him, knocking him away.

The door slammed open, and Anton marched inside. His long black hair was pulled back and his sword was drawn. Fire flared in his red eyes. He was terrifying enough, but it was the long blond-haired man wearing a red and black flannel shirt and jeans that emitted an ethereal power. White light flickered around him and he unsheathed his sword.

No fear shone in his eyes. "Be gone, Balthazar." His voice was loud and authoritative.

The black wolf snarled and then shifted into the same shirtless demon I had seen in my dream.

Same long, black hair.

Same bulking muscles.

Same evil power.

My wolf was definitely ten times braver than me. I was cowering, but she refused to step down.

Balthazar flicked his gaze over Raphael. "Ah, Raphael, you actually came to challenge me."

Raphael? Like the Archangel Raphael?

Raphael flashed him a daring smile. "Yes, I did."

"You think you and that vampire are strong enough to banish me?"

"No," a commanding voice said behind me. "But I am." The loud voice had a power that demanded obedience.

Luna, Remus, and I looked behind us, and I instinctively retreated. A man with long, dark hair and a deep scowl emerged from the shadows. He didn't have to say his name. I instantly knew who it was—the Archangel Michael.

He walked toward Balthazar with a glittering sword.

Fear flashed in the demon's red eyes. "No, Michael. You can put away Excalibur." He gestured toward me. "I only came for what belongs to me. That bitch stole them."

My wolf stood in front of Luna and Remus like a shield. I wouldn't allow the demon to ensnare them again.

Michael flashed him a sarcastic smile. "Do you take me for a fool, Balthazar?"

Balthazar slammed his palm on his broad chest. "No. But they are demon wolves. Not angel wolves."

"They were not spawned in Hell. They were born in the Elder Dimension and then you cursed them," Michael said as he edged closer to the demon, who backed up.

Elder Dimension? That sent my head spinning.

Balthazar backed up against a twin bed. "Nevertheless, they are mine and have been for the last hundred years."

Raphael closed in on the demon. "You don't think you can actually stop the prophecy, do you?"

Balthazar pointed at me. "You'll pay for this, Wolf Princess. All those you hold dear will perish. Every. Last. One."

With that, he vanished, ripping out my heart. Despair crushed my lungs and I couldn't breathe. Mateo…Gunnar… Remi…Quint…

Aaoooo Aaoooo Aaoooo

I howled mournfully. Luna and Remus joined in my sad call.

Raphael sheathed his sword and knelt next to me. "Balthazar is evil, but he isn't strong enough to break the prophecy. I have fortified Legacy so he cannot enter again. Never fear, Princess. The first king's blood flows in your veins and it is time for you to fulfill your destiny. Remember, you're not alone in this war."

He joined Michael and the two of them faded away into a bright ball of light that glided out the window.

Anton looked at me and smiled. "Salem, we need to talk. Are you able?"

My wolf hung her head, and I shifted.

Dr. Greenwood rushed over with a blanket and wrapped me in it. "Thank you for saving my life. Thank your wolves, too."

I tightened the fluffy blanket around me. "And you for saving me."

"It was an honor." He gestured for me to go with Anton.

The ancient vampire rubbed his beard. "You can't cross the snowy courtyard wearing only a blanket. I will send clothes for you and then you will dine with me."

I frowned. "What about my own clothes and the Book of Goody? Was Michael right? Are the demon wolves from the Elder Dimension?"

"I will answer all your questions in good time." He glanced down at Luna and Remus. "And of course these two are welcome in my home as well. They haven't left you for these past few days."

I frowned. "Days? Oh, and the others? My friends?"

"Yes, days. Your friends are fine. They have been worried sick about you and they've been at your side the whole time. Now they are all getting some much-needed rest."

I looked out the windows where the angels had gone and saw the sun was sneaking up the mountains.

Anton smiled brightly. "Dawn is approaching." He bowed slightly. "A new era is about to begin. I will explain everything soon."

With that, he left, leaving me with more questions than answers.

10

Thirty minutes later, I was dressed in a heavy white sweater, black jeans and high boots, walking across the snowy courtyard to Anton's home with Luna and Remus on either side of me. His home was a tall tower with a wraparound balcony at the top that allowed him to see all of Legacy.

His wasn't the only tower. There were five others that served as the dormitory for each of the supernatural bloodlines—Wyvern for the dragons, Shadow for the vampires, Mystic for the Golden Demons, Glamour for the Fae, and Pack for the wolves. I stared at the Pack Tower with its blue flag fluttering proudly at the top of its turret, wishing I could forget everything and attend school here with my demon wolves and Mateo at my side.

Students were already up and looking at us questioningly. I envied them. Because of my uncle, I couldn't ever attend Legacy, and even if I became queen, I still wouldn't be able to. I wondered if they realized how lucky they were. If I did win this fight against Calvin, I wanted to make sure that my future kingdom had an academy. If there already was one, I doubted if it was running like Anton did Legacy. He was just as Ashton and Ebony had always described him—cryptic and mysterious.

That's who I would like to be in charge of ours.

Ebony had said the angels were dicks, but that wasn't what I saw. They'd been there when I needed them. How had Anton contacted them? Were they friends?

Anton opened the door to his home as if he knew I was coming.

He stretched out his arm. "Good morning, Salem. We're all waiting for you."

I smiled. "Morning."

Luna and Remus bounded inside and looked around, checking to see if it was safe for me to come inside. Remus snarled. I chuckled. That meant Hades must be inside. I brushed past Anton. Sure enough, Hades and Remus were already squaring off. Hades was in front of Ebony, who was curled up on a red leather couch, drinking a cup of coffee. I had the feeling Remus wouldn't be satisfied until he bested Hades, which was impossible. Hades might have been slightly smaller, but he was a powerful Catalan dragon that sparked fear even in the Unseelie.

I snapped my fingers. "Remus, no."

Remus turned his head and looked at me balefully.

"Come and sit next to Luna."

He snapped one more time at Hades, who released a menacing growl, then reluctantly sat next to Luna.

Ebony put her cup of coffee down on a mahogany end table and rubbed Hades' mane. "I guess they're never going to be buds, huh?"

I shook my head as I scratched Remus' ear. "Not anytime soon."

Ashton strode into the room with Gloria. They had cups of coffee in their hands. The man behind me drew my attention. He was as tall as Anton, or maybe even taller. His long black hair was pulled up in a man bun and his rugged beard and mustache made him look like a real badass.

He bowed slightly. "It's nice to finally meet you, Princess. I'm Stefan Gabor, Headmaster and Warden of Hollows Academy."

"Just Salem, please," I whispered.

So this was the dude that my aunt had a crush on. I could see why. He could probably just look at a woman and get her to take off her panties. But what was he doing here? I glanced at Ebony, who was blinking away tears. Crap, this had to have something to do with Gunnar.

Anton rubbed his hands together. "Good." He headed toward a room that was off the living room. "Since everyone is here, I suggest we adjourn to the dining room, where a feast has been prepared for all of you."

His home was as I remembered it—decorated Dracula-style with long red velvet drapes, hardwood floors, and red leather couches and chairs. If no one knew Anton was a vampire, they would guess it based on his decor.

The smell coming from the dining room was heavenly—bacon, eggs, coffee, and freshly baked bread. My mouth watered and I could hardly wait to fill my empty belly. It took everything I had not to stampede in there, knocking everyone down.

The table was elegantly set with a white linen tablecloth and looked like something out of a fine dining restaurant, with candles glittering in gold candelabras, matching china dishes, and crystal glasses. On a buffet table were silver chafing dishes. My attention was riveted on the silver coffeepot and I made my way over to it.

Whatever Anton and Stefan were going to lay on me, I would need coffee first, and lots of it.

Anton gestured toward the buffet table. "Please, everyone help yourself. Cook has prepared bacon, sausage, homemade biscuits and gravy, and scrambled eggs."

Hades, Luna, and Remus all looked at him with big, soulful eyes.

Anton laughed. "Don't worry. Cook is preparing something special for you three, too."

Just as he said that, two men came bustling into the room carrying big bowls of steaming beef.

They set them on the ground a little away from the dining room table. "Help yourselves."

But they were too close together. Hades and Remus would definitely get in a fight over whose was whose. I grabbed one of the bowls and moved it close to where Ebony was sitting. Hades loved Ebony.

"Here's yours, little buddy."

He glared at the two wolves but happily came over to Ebony, who winked at me.

I picked up a coffee cup, filled it with the steaming brew, and doctored it with lots of cream. I placed it on the table and then grabbed a plate, ready to load it up. My tummy growled, demanding food, food, food.

Anton's cook had outdone himself. By the time I sat down, my plate was loaded to the gills with crispy bacon, country sausage, scrambled eggs, hash browns, and two biscuits coated with gravy.

"Hungry?" Anton smiled as he filled my glass three quarters of the way with champagne and then topped it off with fresh squeezed orange juice.

"Starving." I placed a napkin on my lap.

"Good. We have plenty to talk about—and celebrate."

I wasn't sure what the celebration was for, but I'm sure Anton would spill the beans soon. I wanted to dive into my plate and sip my mimosa, but I forced myself to wait until Anton finally finished filling everyone's glasses and sat down.

"I'd like to propose a toast to Salem."

Everyone raised their glasses.

He smiled at me. "For freeing not one but two demon wolves from the Unseelie curse."

"Hear, hear," everyone echoed.

Heat spread over my face. I wasn't used to such praise and my cheeks turned warm. I quickly grabbed my water glass to douse the burning inside me.

"Thank you," I mumbled.

Anton lowered his glass and placed his napkin in his lap. "Now, it's time for Salem to learn why she's the chosen one, and how the demon wolves are connected with her."

All of us stared at him. I held my breath, not sure what to expect.

"I'm afraid much of the lore of the Moon Kingdom has been lost for many years." He picked up a piece of bacon and took a small bite. "Even I cannot remember the legends."

I sat on the edge of my chair, my food and drink forgotten.

He turned to me as he took a sip of his mimosa. "Tell me, Salem, have you ever wondered why you were able to break the demon wolves' Unseelie curse?"

I glanced around at all my friends. "Because of the Book of Goody?" My voice was unsure and slow.

I didn't understand why he was saying this, since he was the one who had the Book of Goody.

Ashton cocked his eyebrow. "Secrets again, Anton?"

"Not so much secrets as a reminder—from the Archangel Raphael."

A quiver of fear raced down my spine. "Wh-wh-what do you mean by that?"

He smiled as he cut up his biscuits and gravy. "What the Archangel Michael said was true—the demon wolves are not from Hell."

Gloria frowned. "Then where do they come from?"

"The Elder Dimension," Anton said.

Ashton's mouth dropped open. "You're kidding."

"No, I'm not. And there's more. There's a reason Salem has bonded with the wolves. There's a reason she's the chosen one."

Stefan leaned closer. "And that is?"

"The first king's parents. His father was a wolf shifter, as are most of you, but his mother was an Unseelie from the Elder Dimension. She gave demon wolf pups to her son, and they formed a close alliance."

The blood drained from my face. "I have Unseelie blood? No, that can't be true."

Anton recited on as if he hadn't heard me, like he was giving a lecture. "The first king's mother had green eyes, same as the first king. And now you."

I was still trying to see how one and one equaled four, but Anton's math was way over my head. I rubbed my slick forehead. "But how can this be? There have been other kings since the first king, and they would have had the Unseelie blood—"

"True," Anton said. "But they were not chosen."

"But Mom had green eyes just like mine."

He smiled. "I know. But all this comes from your father's bloodline, not your mother's. According to the Archangel Raphael, you were chosen, and this is your destiny."

Ebony's eyes widened. "You mean Heaven actually cares? Rusty said that the angels would never help."

Stefan snorted. "Rusty and the angels don't exactly see eye to eye. Truth is, the last thing the angels want is for Balthazar to regain control of the demon wolves. He uses them to hunt down innocent souls that are destined for Heaven."

Gloria poured more cream into her coffee. "What do you mean?"

Stefan's eyes darkened, and then he twirled the stem of his wineglass. "He's even used them to kill reapers."

Luna and Remus whimpered and slumped down on the floor as if they felt guilty.

Stefan looked over at them. "I do not consider you two personally responsible. I hold Balthazar and Velkan accountable for your behavior."

I wasn't sure if I believed him, but regardless, I couldn't allow him to hurt my wolves. I patted my thigh to make sure they stayed close by. "You really don't blame them?"

He flashed me a surly smile. "No, I don't. Demon wolves…let's just say they aren't the only ones who can be cursed."

I gulped and glanced around my team. They all had the same startled look as I did. What had happened to this dude?

Stefan leaned back in his chair. "But we're not here to talk about me. I'm here to ask for all of your help, because we have a serious problem."

I frowned. "What?"

Ebony blurted, "Gunnar's sister Kara and her friend Killian have escaped from the Hollows."

Stefan sighed heavily. "And they had help. Calvin's special forces."

Crap. Not good. "Was it just Kara and Killian who escaped?"

Say yes Say yes Say yes Say yes

"No. They weren't. They freed two of the most evil Dark Demons locked up in my cells."

"You're not saying…you're not saying…don't tell me…" Ebony stammered. Her face turned white as her hair.

"Yeah, I am." Stefan drained his mimosa. "Faas and Ari are gone."

An eerie, sinking feeling plopped in my gut. "Who are Faas and Ari?"

Stefan looked at me. "It's not as much who they are as what they can do. Faas can throw fireballs."

My eyes widened. "Seriously?"

"And he's not even the worst one." Stefan tapped his fingers. "Ari has long, poisonous nails, and can shift into anything. He's extremely dangerous."

I scrubbed my face.

This was bad.

This was my worst nightmare bad.

This was I'm-going-to-get-my-ass-kicked bad.

11

No one spoke at the breakfast table. Suddenly, food didn't seem so important. I took a deep breath and shoved my plate away.

Anton looked down at my plate and then up at me reprovingly. "You need to eat."

The last thing I wanted was food. Burning bile rose up my throat. I put my elbows on the table and rested my forehead in my palms. "I've lost my appetite. So, tell me—do you think Calvin has recruited these two dark demons to kill me?"

"Perhaps. Right now, he's desperate and dangerous," he said.

I put my arms down. "So what do I do now?"

"You fight him," Ebony said. "Calvin's only doing this because he's afraid of you. You have the power to take away his crown."

"Is she strong enough yet to face Ari and Faas? They have killed the strongest and bravest warriors," Stefan asked gravely. His tone was like a skeletal hand squeezing my heart tighter and tighter.

Anton pushed away his empty plate with finality. "She will be if she can find the Rose Box and discover its secrets. Time is essential. You must find it before Calvin recruits additional powerful supernaturals."

"Well, that's a problem, since he has the baddest army around. Plus, I have no idea where the Rose Box is, and in the meantime, Mateo, Gunnar, and everyone else were being strung up by their Buster Browns." I couldn't keep the bitterness and anger out of my voice.

Anton didn't seem the slightest bit annoyed by my tone. He smiled briefly and reached over and petted Luna. "Your demon wolves know."

She wagged her tail, thumping it hard on the hardwood floor.

I glanced down at her. "You really know where it is, girl?"

She placed her head in my lap and looked up at me with sweet puppy eyes. Remus nudged me and wagged his tail, giving me the same soulful look.

Gloria put her elbows on the table and rested her chin in her palms as she looked between them curiously. "Weird. It's almost as if they understand you, Salem."

"It's because they do," Anton said simply.

I stroked the top of their heads and grinned. "I always thought they did."

"You're connected," Stefan said. "They'll be able to lead you to the Rose Box…" he waved his finger in a circle "…*if* you're hunting in the right place."

"But it could be anywhere!" Ashton threw up his hands. "We could be running around for ages before we stumbled on it."

"Salem, you need to ask the wolves where it is," Anton urged.

I rolled my eyes. "But I don't speak wolf."

"Try. Ask them yes or no questions. It's a place to start." His voice was mesmerizing. I couldn't resist.

"Here goes nothing," I mumbled. "Luna, Remus, did Velkan hide the Rose Box near Hayley's home?"

Luna wagged her tail, and Remus growled, his hackles standing straight up.

Gloria frowned. "What's that supposed to mean?"

"This is ridiculous," Ashton grumbled.

"Ignore him." Anton motioned with his hand and gave Ashton a sharp look. "Try again."

I studied them. Luna had been with me longer than Remus. What if Velkan had moved it since Luna had been with Velkan and she didn't know?

Feeling like it was a long shot, I forced myself to ask, "Remus, did Velkan move the Rose Box?"

He thumped his tail eagerly.

This totally blew my mind. "Wow, he really does understand."

"That really proves nothing." Ashton slapped his palm on the table.

His doubting Thomas routine was getting to me. I glared. "Do you have any better ideas?"

Ashton slumped down in his chair and scowled. "No. I don't."

I thought of all the places where Velkan could hide the Rose Box, and all signs pointed to one place. "Remus, did Velkan take the Rose Box back to Iredale Palace?"

He thumped his tail.

"Do you know where it is?"

He licked my hand.

I looked around the circle. "I suppose that means yes." I stroked the top of his head and sat forward eagerly. "Is it in Calvin's bedroom?"

Remus sat perfectly still and stopped licking my hand.

"Well, I guess that's a big fat no." I tapped my chin. "What about Calvin's torture chamber?"

Once again, he didn't move.

"You could be asking him all night," Stefan said gently. "The best and much faster thing to do would be to go to Iredale Palace and allow the wolf to show you where the demon hid the box."

I slapped my thighs. "Right. This is it." I looked at everyone. "We're going in."

"I believe the time is right," Anton said, nodding. "Once your crown is restored, you'll be able to reclaim Iredale and return the palace to its glory."

"But what about Kara and Killian, Headmaster?" Ebony asked. "Do you think they are at Iredale Palace, or Abbadon Rock?"

"Hard to say." Anton rubbed his beard. "But I don't believe they would go to Abbadon Rock. That's the royal seat. The Dark Demons wouldn't accept Kara as queen unless they had absolute proof Gunnar was dead. No, I believe they will go to Iredale Palace."

"To kill Gunnar," Ebony choked on the words. She inhaled and exhaled deeply. "Salem's right. Our path is leading to Iredale Palace."

Gloria bit her lip and hugged her waist. "They'll kill us when we attack, do you think?"

"Maybe." I pushed my hair behind my ears. "They'll be expecting us."

Anton sighed and fixed his dark eyes on me. "He'd be a fool if he wasn't." His dry voice made me break out in goosebumps.

Ashton gritted his teeth. "Did it ever occur to any of you we could be walking into a trap?" He pointed his finger down on the table for emphasis. "That this is exactly what Calvin wants."

"We can't fight him alone," I said. "He's gathering an army."

Ashton stiffened. "My father pledged to fight this war."

"But your father isn't enough," I said glumly.

Anton wiped his mouth with his cloth napkin. "I think I will be able to persuade King Erick of the Timber Kingdom to align with us. His son, Xavier, attended Legacy."

"Rusty and Julie will help, too," Stefan said.

"What about the angels?" Ebony asked quietly. By her tone, she didn't think the angels would lift one finger.

"Trust me," Stefan said. "They will if Balthazar gets involved. Michael and Balthazar have an ancient feud."

I flashed him a sarcastic smile. “Based on what I saw in the infirmary, they’re already involved.”

“You would think so,” Stefan mused. “But you can’t be sure. The archangels have their own agenda and only do what they believe is destined.”

“So,” I drawled out the word and placed my hand on my chest. “Me being the Queen of the Moon Kingdom, they wouldn’t believe that was destiny?”

Stefan shrugged. “Like I said, we don’t know.”

Anton pushed my plate toward me. “Before you do anything, you need to eat. You’re running on empty. You can’t afford to make any mistakes now, Salem. Too many lives are at stake.” He pointed at my plate. “And going into battle with an empty belly would be beyond foolish.”

I wanted to argue that I wasn’t hungry, but my gut betrayed me and growled loudly.

Anton cocked his eyebrow as if daring me to defy him.

I dragged my plate back toward me and forced myself to eat. The scrambled eggs and gravy had gotten cold, but my belly didn’t care.

“Tomorrow, you need to make your way to Iredale Palace,” Anton said. “You must be careful. Calvin will be having the roads watched.”

Ebony lifted her chin high scornfully. “An ambush?”

“Fairness has never been high on Calvin’s agenda,” Ashton smirked.

“Nevertheless, his attack will be well planned.” Anton waved his finger. “Don’t underestimate him. He’s ruthless.”

Ashton narrowed his eyes. “You don’t have to tell me that. I’m very well acquainted with how ruthless Calvin can be to those he believes have betrayed him.” His ominous tone made me think of Mateo and how he must be suffering—no food, no water, no mercy—while I was indulging in a breakfast fit for a queen.

Still a chewing on a piece of crispy bacon, I looked down at my food and my appetite disappeared again.

Ebony wiped tears from her cheeks. "We have to go soon. I can't stop thinking about Gunnar. He's suffered so much." She bit her lip. "The things that his father did to him…and now Calvin…" Her horns rose out of her head, and she got up abruptly from the table. "If you'll excuse me."

She headed out of the dining room.

Hades hurried after her, his tail twitching back and forth.

I got up from the table. "I'd better go talk to her."

Anton shook his head and clasped my hand. "No, let her be. Hades will comfort her. She needs to gather her wits about her. You have a valuable ally in that one. She's more than just a vampire."

"I know." I frowned. "How are you going to convince the other wolf kingdoms to join us?"

"I'll show you after you're done eating."

I scooted my chair back. "I'm full. Truly I am. I'd like you to show me now."

"Very well. Come with me." He stood and gestured with his arm. "Please, all of you, follow me."

Anton led us up to his balcony and opened the door, smiling like the cat who just stole the very best cream.

My mouth dropped open as my demon wolves raced out in front of me. Freedom sat perched on the balcony railing.

"Oh, my God." I smiled and clapped my hands. "Freedom."

He tipped his head back and forth when he saw me. The wolves sat on either side of him.

"Well, well." Ashton cast his gaze over the giant eagle. "So, this is the famous Freedom. I have to say, he's quite impressive."

Stefan looked at Anton. "How did you manage to bring him here? A compulsion spell?"

Anton shook his head. "No. It wasn't me, I can assure you." He looked over at me. "I believe he was following our princess."

I admired the beautiful eagle. He was magnificent. "But why would he care about me?"

"Because I believe he thinks all the pieces of the wolf princess puzzle are falling into place. He's waiting for you to free his beloved mistress."

I glanced over at Anton and crinkled my brows. "You mean Hayley?"

"Yes." The ancient vampire stroked the giant bird of prey's beak without fear. "Just as Hades is attached to Gunnar, and the demon wolves are bonded with you, Freedom is devoted to Hayley. Witches and their familiars have very powerful bonds and these two have been separated for far too long."

I petted Luna's back. "Did you use the *Curasi Perfio* spell on Freedom?"

Anton dropped his hand. "No. That's an Unseelie spell. I know another one that the High Priestess of Good Academy taught me —the *Exculsi* spell—that is not so intrusive or forceful. The familiar may choose whether they want to become human temporarily, while the *Curasi Perfio* spell forces them."

"It does?" I put my hands on my hips. "I didn't know that. Now I feel terrible. Why on Earth didn't you tell me the last time I was here?"

"Because I didn't know. I visited Goody Magic Academy recently and that's when the High Priestess taught me the spell."

"Why did you go there?"

He chuckled. "I wanted to check on, ahh, an old friend—the new dishwasher in the girls' dormitory."

That sounded strange. I frowned. "Really? Why?"

He covered his mouth as if to hide a smile. "Because he's been giving a certain reaper fits."

"I'm not sure Rusty would find that amusing," Anton warned.

"Oh, I know he wouldn't, but I just can't help it. Jaxon has given him the slip more than once."

"Is this guy Jaxon a reaper?" Ashton asked.

"No, he's a vampire that got himself into big trouble." Anton put his hands behind his back and looked over the balcony at a few students who were crossing the snowy courtyard. Anton reminded of an eagle himself, guarding his eaglets. "Let's just say it's his penance."

"Whatever that means," Ashton murmured.

I looked at Freedom and placed my hand on my chest.. "I'm truly sorry if I hurt you when I used the *Curasi Perfio* spell." A lump of guilt formed in my dry throat. "I didn't know."

The eagle inclined his head, and I hoped that meant I was forgiven. I hesitantly petted his feathers, and he didn't snap at me. I was surprised at how soft they were. Then he twitched his head to straighten his feathers, and I decided not to push my luck.

I stood next to Anton with my wolves behind me. They were so loyal. Tomorrow, the final battle was about to begin.

New enemies had been added to our fight, but we had reapers on our side now. I had no idea if reapers could cancel out a demon who threw fireballs or one with evil nails, but I'd take any help I could get.

Stay alive, Mateo. I'm coming.

12

Morning came way too soon for my liking. Sleep had eluded me and I had thrashed on my bed all night long, thoughts of my uncle, Mateo, and the Rose Box swirling in my head. Was I was strong enough to beat my uncle and bust my mate out of his twisted fun house? Right now, he and I were evenly matched with our demon wolves. He had two, and I had two, but to win, I would have to have all four—plus steal the Rose Box from him.

Definitely mission impossible, but I had to try. If I didn't, then my douchebag uncle would continue to kill everyone I loved.

I sighed heavily and sat up, rubbing my eyes. My demon wolves were curled up next to each other, sleeping about a foot away from my bed. They looked so happy and peaceful. If I wasn't able to break the Unseelie curse on my uncle's wolves, then Remus and Luna would be forced to fight their siblings. That would break my heart.

I crawled out from underneath my thick quilt, careful not to disturb them. They needed their rest before we set out on our desperate journey. I snuck into the bathroom and quietly shut the door. I wanted to have one last long, hot shower before I set out to meet my uncle. Who knew when I would have another one?

I turned lazily in the warm water, lathering my hair, soaping my body, wishing Mateo was with here with me. God, I missed him so much that it hurt.

Only once the water ran cold did I step out and dry myself with a luxurious, thick red towel. I quickly combed out my hair and washed my face. God, I looked like death warmed over with my bloodshot eyes and the dark shadows underneath them. I put concealer underneath my eyes, but it really didn't do crap. Even after applying some blush and mauve lip gloss, I still looked like a ghastly ghost.

I dressed in a heavy black sweater, pair of jeans, and tall, soft sheepskin boots. Next, I placed a change of clothes on top of the Book of Goody. I debated whether I should even bring it, since my uncle so desperately wanted it, but I had a feeling I might need it.

The demon wolves were up now and pacing by the bedroom door. I flung my backpack over my shoulder and smiled at the pair of them. "So, you two are excited about the journey?" I asked as I opened it.

The two of them raced out, with me behind them.

Grrrrr Snarrrrl

I rolled my eyes. Remus must have run smack into Hades. Would those two ever get along? I was beginning to doubt it.

When I walked into the living room, sure enough, the two of them were squaring off, their hackles up, ears flattened, and upper lips pulled back, revealing sharp teeth.

I pointed at the floor. "Remus, come."

Remus didn't move.

I snapped my fingers and raised my voice. "Remus, come. *Now*."

The wolf slowly backed away from Hades and sat next to me obediently, but he was still growling.

I looked at the little Catalan dragon. "Hades, stay."

I stood between them. "Listen to me. You two need to stop fighting. We're going into battle and we need to work as a team. Otherwise, Calvin wins."

They each bowed their heads miserably, as if they had understood my every word.

Ebony entered the living room and laughed. "Those two at it again?"

I nodded and rolled my eyes. "Of course."

Just like me, she had dark circles underneath her bloodshot eyes.

"Did you get any sleep at all?" I asked softly.

"Not much." She yawned and covered her mouth. "You?"

"Hardly any."

Ebony stroked Hades' mane. "Hey, buddy." She turned back to me and gave me a weary smile. "I just couldn't stop thinking about Gunnar and what they could be doing to him." A tear slid down her cheek and she hurriedly brushed it away. "I promised myself I wouldn't cry anymore, but..." She cleared her throat. "When I think how many Dark Demons want him dead, and what Calvin does to traitors..." Her voice trailed off, and she turned away.

"I know. But we'll get Mateo and Gunnar out of that place alive. I swear." I slowly approached her. "Hug?"

"Yes." She opened her arms wide. "I would like that."

We hugged each other tightly as if we would never see each other again. Her heart was pounding as fiercely as mine.

"You two ready?" Ashton came into the living room with his backpack flung over his shoulder.

I untangled myself from Ebony and sighed. "Ready as we're ever gonna be."

Ashton tilted his head. "Make sure you grab some grub before we go. The Moon Kingdom is high in the mountains and the road is usually closed this time of year. We'll leave my car at the scenic overlook on Trail Ridge Road and hike in from there. Moon Kingdom's about fifty miles north."

Ouch. Fifty miles?

Anton came into the living room. "Breakfast is ready. Today isn't as fancy as it was yesterday, but we have bagels and cream cheese, chocolate croissants, and bacon. Cook has also packed a knapsack full of fried chicken sandwiches, bananas, and nuts. You'll need it as you cross the pass." His face turned grim. "You also need to be careful. They'll be expecting you, and I suspect you will be ambushed." His solemn words had me wondering if we would even make it to the kingdom alive.

"How long do you think it will take us to get to the Moon Kingdom?" I wasn't looking forward to hiking through the snow, but I would do anything to save Mateo.

Ashton shrugged. "In our human forms, it would take us at least three or four days to get there. Quicker if we go as wolves."

"Then that's what we do." Not that tearing off my warm sweater and jeans out in a winter storm was appealing.

He smiled happily. "Suits me fine. I'm looking forward to a winter run."

Ebony cocked her eyebrow. "Since I'm not a wolf, I guess I get to carry the food and everyone's backpack?"

"Yup, you do, but I don't think your huge bat will have a problem carrying them, do you?" Ashton smiled.

Hades thumped his tail.

She smiled. "Going to help me, buddy? Thanks."

He nudged her hand.

Ebony headed toward the kitchen. "I'm starved. Let's eat."

We followed her into the dining room, and I headed straight for the coffeepot.

Gloria strolled into the dining room, yawning. Unlike Ebony and me, she didn't look like she'd tossed and turned all night. She looked as beautiful as ever and her makeup was perfect, from her gold flickering eyeshadow down to her pink lipstick that matched her lacy collared sweater.

"Wakey, wakey," I said as I sipped my coffee loaded with cream.

She held up a finger. "Give me a minute. I couldn't sleep last night, knowing I'd be facing my dad again."

Really? God, I wished l looked like that when I hadn't slept.

I stopped spreading cream cheese on my bagel and set it down. Ebony and I glanced at each other. "We won't let him hurt you, Gloria."

"We promise," Ebony chimed in. She hugged Gloria. "We're the three Vindicator sisters."

Gloria nodded and even smiled, but I could see it in her eyes. She was scared shitless.

"Gloria, you don't have to do this," I said gently. "You could stay here with Anton and be safe. There's no shame in staying behind."

She raised her head defiantly. "I may be frightened of my father, but I'm not chickening out," she snapped. "I'm part of this team. Plus, I know the castle better than any of you. You need me."

I frowned, not sure where this sudden anger was coming from. "Calm down, Gloria. Of course we need you."

She stood straighter and gave each of us a sour look. "It's just everyone looks at me like I'm just a stupid, pretty princess. I'm not. I'm not an idiot."

I cocked my head and smiled at her. "No. You're absolutely not. You're the reason Ashton and I were able to escape from Iredale Palace. And I'll tell you a secret, girl—you're not the only one who is scared. We all are."

Ebony winked at her. "So, don't sweat it."

Gloria gave us a grateful smile and wiped her sweaty palms on her back denim jeans. "Thanks. Sorry." She took a deep breath and exhaled. "Well, I guess I'd better eat."

The last to come into the dining room was Stefan. He looked as handsome as usual, with his long dark hair pulled into a man bun, and he wasn't alone. A tall, good-looking guy with red hair and a bandana wrapped around his head held hands with a beautiful blond blue-eyed woman.

Ebony's eyes widened. "Oh, my God. Rusty!"

I choked on my coffee. "Reaper Rusty?" As in the badass with a serious Dean Winchester attitude problem?

"Yeah, what of it?" He gave me a cool look.

I shrugged. "Nothing."

"Rusty, stop." The blonde elbowed him in the ribs.

He frowned at her. "Hey. Watch it, babe."

She gave him a kiss on the cheek. "I'll watch it if you behave." She put her hand on her chest. "I'm Julie Sumner."

"She's been my sister's best friend since grade school," Ebony said as she got up from the table. "I want a hug, bad boy." She ran over to Rusty with her arms spread wide.

Rusty picked her up and swung her around. "Good to see you, girl." He kissed her on the cheek. "I've missed you, too."

"Whoa." Ebony tilted her head back and laughed.

Rusty set her down. "So, I hear I've got to save Gunnar's dumb ass again."

"Hey." Ebony punched him in the arm. "Don't say that."

He grinned. "Hey, you know I like the guy." He looked around. "Did someone say Hades was here? I thought he was always supposed to stay with Gunnar."

Ebony and I looked at each other, and then she cleared her throat. "Gunnar commanded him to protect Salem."

"Figures. Why doesn't the witless wonder command him to come back and save his ass?"

"It's not that easy." Ebony glanced nervously at me and then back at Rusty. "Gunnar told Hades he has to stay with Salem until she's crowned queen."

I could feel the blood drain from my face to my gut. "Wha-at? I didn't know that. You mean if he wasn't bonded to me, he could save Gunnar and Mateo?"

Ebony stared at me. "Gunnar believes in you, Salem. He also knows that Calvin is really evil." She spread her arms. "Look what he's done. Made pacts with demons, the Unseelie, and now he's broken out the two worst demons from the Hollows."

"That's why we're here," Rusty said. "Julie, Stefan, and I will take on Velkan and any other demons lurking around."

"That's not all, though," Ebony said. "Somehow Calvin and the Unseelie have opened a portal to the Elder Dimension and now have harpies on their team."

"As reapers, we don't fear them," Julie said. "But trust me, they will fear us."

Something in her soft tone made the hairs on the back of my neck stand up. I'd never seen reapers fight, but I had a feeling I wouldn't want to meet them in a dark alley.

Stefan put down his cup of coffee. "Julie, Rusty, and I will also return Kara and Killian to the Hollows."

"How did they manage to break out of the Hollows, anyway?" Rusty asked curiously. "When Julie and I were locked up in there, there was no way we could break out."

"With an Unseelie spell that freezes time." He picked up a chocolate croissant. "It also froze me. And I can't have that." A dark shadow fell across his face. "They need to be made an example of." If Kara or Killian had heard the tone of his voice or the fiery look in his eyes, they would have dropped to their knees and begged for mercy.

But I had a feeling maybe they weren't that bright.

"Great," I said in a huff. "Can this Unseelie spell be broken?"

Stefan focused his gaze on me as he swallowed the last bite of his croissant. "Yes." He pointed at me. "But only by you." His low voice scared the pants off me.

Just some more weight piled onto my slender shoulders. "Why me?"

"Because you're descended from the first king. You're the chosen one. Your Unseelie blood will help you break the spell, but you must believe in yourself to do it."

I picked up my backpack and unzipped it. "Do you think I will find the spell in the Book of Goody?"

I can help, the voice said.

"Maybe it's in there," Stefan said slowly. "But I also think you will have to draw on all your power to execute it."

"What if I can't?"

He flashed me a sorrowful smile. "Then we all die."

13

Stefan's bomb about the Unseelie's freezing spell was just another miserable thing added to my plate. I was just a rebellious girl who'd grown up in the foster care system, and suddenly everyone was looking to me as if I was going to transfer into Hermione Granger and save the day.

I placed the Book of Goody on the table and flicked through the pages like a madwoman, hoping to find a thawing spell. Usually my fingers would tingle or the pages would stop when I found the right spell, but this time nothing.

Oh, shit. This wasn't good.

Anton came up alongside me. "Are you finding anything?"

"No. But it's got to be in here. It has to be."

Come on, please, help me book.

But the voice was silent.

Anton's smile did not quite reach both sides of his mouth as he looked at me curiously. "Perhaps you are looking for the wrong spell?"

I immediately stopped flipping through the pages and drew in a deep, startled breath. "Excuse me?"

"You are looking for a spell to counter the freezing spell,

correct?" His tone practically screamed that I had done something terribly wrong.

"Yeah, so?" He was trying my patience. I wished he just spit out what he was trying to say.

He gestured toward the Warden of The Hollows. "Were you not paying attention to Stefan?"

I gritted my teeth. "Yes, I was listening to him."

"And what did he say?" Anton asked patiently.

Everyone was staring at me. I cursed the two hot patches burning on my cheeks. If ever I wanted to strangle anyone, he would be my choice. "He said that I had to draw on my power."

"And that the unfreezing spell might not be in the Book of Goody," he finished for me.

The burning on my cheeks slowly slipped down my neck and spread to every part of my body. My blood burned hotter and my clothes stuck to my skin. What an idiot. I flicked my hair back and slumped down in my chair. "If the spell isn't in here, then what the hell am I supposed to do?"

"Look for another spell. One that increases your power," Anton scratched both Remus' and Luna's ears, "and draws on the demon wolves' power. Like the first king, Salem, you are connected to the demon wolves. Something that your uncle never will be. This power did not pass on to him. It passed to you."

"I don't understand. How can I draw on the demon wolves' power? I didn't even know they had power."

"Ah, but they do," he said. "They are from the Elder Dimension and possess a magic that has yet to be unleashed. I believe your uncle knows this, and he's been combing every nook and cranny in our world looking for a solution. That is why he imprisoned Hayley. His attempts to force her to tell him the secret of controlling the wolves have failed. That's why he has now turned to Balthazar and the Unseelie.

"You think the answer is in the Rose Box, don't you?" I asked.

"I do. But until you uncover the box, look for a spell that

draws other magic to you or enhances your own. If you're powerful enough, any freezing spell Calvin or the Unseelie cast on you won't work."

I glanced at Stefan, who was obviously very strong. "But Stefan is powerful, and it froze him."

"I am powerful, yes," Stefan said. "But absorbing magic from others is a gift I do not possess. In fact, I only know one other person who can do this."

My brows crinkled. "Who?"

"My sister, Raven," Ebony said quietly. "She not only can draw on the magic of others but also use their own magic against them. But it took her a long time to learn how."

"Plus, Raven went to school here for four years, plus she's the most powerful supernatural being in our world," I said glumly. I was so screwed.

"Everything you said is true," Anton said. "But. Raven doesn't possess Unseelie blood, nor does she have a connection with demon wolves. You do. It's not the same as Raven's significant gifts, but do not underestimate its power."

He was such a Mr. Sunshine about this, and I was a Cloudy Clara. It was overwhelming. It felt like an avalanche of problems kept smashing into me. "But how am I supposed to master this connection, Anton?"

"You are already on the path, Salem. You have broken the curse on two of the demon wolves and they are not only loyal to you, but they understand you. Thus, I believe your wolf may even possess some demon wolf blood."

"I'm not sure I can do it."

"Yes, you can." He gestured to the Book of Goody. "This time, ask for a combining spell. It just may surprise you."

I wasn't sure I believed him, but I didn't want to let my team down, or, worse, fail to rescue Mateo and the others. Maybe this was what I needed to do to be finally one up on Calvin.

Look and believe, the familiar voice said.

"You can do this," Ebony said.

Rusty gave me a don't-be-a-pussy stare while Julie cast me a sympathetic look. It was so strange that these two were together. Talk about opposites attracting.

Ashton and Stefan just looked at me, waiting for me to do something besides whine.

I took a deep breath and once again flipped through the pages. Nothing happened until I was almost at the end of the book. Then tingles started flicking around the tip of my fingers when I was on almost the very last page. Pink swirls swooshed around.

"Whoa. Never seen that before," Rusty muttered.

"She does it all the time," Ashton shrugged. "You get used to it."

I scanned the page. "*Petriendo*. According to this, it's a magic energy absorption spell. The user can absorb magical energy into their body and use it either to enhance their own magic or transfer it to some other object, but there are limitations. The user might be a limit on how much of the magic energy they can consume, and they might have to touch the object to transfer the power to it. Oh, and it says to return the power to the original supernatural, the user must say *Transes*."

Anton studied me. "I believe you will become more powerful each time you use the spell. Why don't you practice it right now?"

"Now?" I asked uneasily.

"Yes. On Remus and Luna."

I bit my lip. "What if it makes me weak, like the *Morphello Refulsi* spell?"

"There's only one way to find out," Anton said.

"But we're about to go into battle," I protested.

"Would you really rather try this for the first time on the battlefield?" Annoyance crept into Anton's voice, as if he was tiring of my excuses.

I stood and looked at my two sweet wolves, who looked at me curiously. "Should I touch them first?"

"I would start there," Anton said. "You might not have to, as you become more familiar with the spell."

I sat between them with my legs crossed. "It won't hurt them, will it?"

He frowned. "I don't believe so, but spells can be tricky."

"Okay, here's goes nothing." I gently rested my palms on my demon wolves' backs. In a loud, clear voice, I said, "*Petriendo.*"

Tingling sensations moved across my fingers like a gliding feather, and something soft slid up my arm. Power pulsed through me faster and faster. My wolf wanted out—now. There was no stopping her. I tilted my head back and arched my spine.

Aaaaaaaooo

My muscles rippled and bulked. The fabric of my jeans tore. My sweater unraveled and fell off me. Fur sprouted all over me. She burst through with a vengeance.

Immediately, I could sense power pulsing through me as if I had just changed into Superman. My wolf wanted to run to test out the new, bigger me, but I wasn't so sure.

Not yet.

Not until I knew what had just happened.

"Shit," Rusty murmured. "That's the biggest damn wolf I've ever seen."

Everyone looked at me uneasily except for Anton, who didn't look the slightest bit perturbed. He got up from the table and calmly refilled his coffee cup.

He looked over the rim of his cup. "She's a dire wolf. Much bigger than your normal wolves."

Ashton frowned. "Wait. Where did the demon wolves go?"

I looked for Remus and Luna, and they were gone. Panic seized me and I whirled around, chasing my tail. Where were my wolves?

Anton glanced around the room and then back at me. Once again, he wasn't astonished.

Gloria gasped and covered her mouth with her palms. "Oh, my God, Salem. Your eyes are red."

Something cold nudged me, and I froze.

Then something soft licked my cheek.

I sniffed, and a familiar scent washed over me.

My demon wolves were right next to me, but they were invisible.

I caught a glimpse of myself in a mirror hanging on the wall and realized Rusty was right. I was a damn big wolf. Taller and broader than normal.

"Anton, what's happening?" Stefan asked.

Anton cocked his eyebrow. "Interesting. You can't see the demon wolves?"

Stefan blinked. "What? No. Are you saying they're invisible?"

"Not to me," Anton said. "But apparently they are to the rest of you." He looked at me curiously. "Can you see them, Salem?"

I couldn't believe it. Anton could see my demon wolves, but I couldn't? How was that even possible?

Concentrate, the voice whispered in my ear.

I inhaled and exhaled deeply until my heart stopped running around like Chicken Little in my chest.

Two outlines formed of my wolves. It was as if someone had sketched them in pencil. Their eyes were no longer red. They looked at me with worried looks.

I walked across the room, and they followed me. Hades joined us and I knew right away he could see them. Remus gnashed his teeth at him and Hades snarled back.

Ebony stared at us with a completely bewildered look on her face. "Anton, can Hades see the demon wolves?"

Anton smiled, and his eyes twinkled. "Yes, I believe he can."

Ashton's scowled deepened. "What does that mean?"

Anton winked at me. "It means when Salem faces her uncle in the arena, she won't be alone."

Was that true? What about Calvin's two demon wolves? Could they see mine? So many questions ran through my head. I thought about shifting, but my clothes were shredded on the floor, even my boots. I grabbed my backpack from the chair with my mouth and then headed out of the room to go change, with my pack following me.

Transes, I whispered in my mind.

Sensations whooshed over me and I shifted back faster than I ever had before. I quickly opened up my backpack and threw on some new clothes. I didn't know what I was going to do about my boots, since I had ripped through those, but I could worry about that later.

Remus and Luna reappeared, looking the same as they had before.

Anton came out of the dining room. "Ah, I see you are back, Salem. How are you feeling?"

I shrugged. "Same as always, but when I was my wolf, I felt like a super wolf. My wolf wanted to test out the new and improved model and go for a run, but I wasn't so sure."

"You have questions, I'm sure." He looked down at my sock feet. "Luckily for you, I have another pair of soft winter boots that Raven left here. Otherwise, you'd have to wear your tennis shoes, and that wouldn't be good hiking through the snow."

Ebony came out of the dining room next. She ran her gaze over me anxiously. "I wanted to make sure you were okay."

I grinned. "I'm fine. Thanks."

"Since your boots are shredded, I have an extra pair if you want to borrow them, if Raven's don't work." She tilted her head back toward the dining room. Then she glanced at Luna and Remus. "They seem to be okay, too."

"Of course they are." Anton returned with the boots.

I quickly put the boots on. They fit just fine. "How do you know?"

"I've been a vampire for a very long time, Salem, and I have read a great many books on the Unseelie. When you used the *Petriendo* spell, you called upon the power of the demon wolves. Usually, the spell would drain a supernatural in our world, but the demon wolves are not of our world, and thus they turned invisible when you borrowed their power."

I leaned back on the couch. "What about the other two demon wolves? If I use the spell against Calvin, will they be able to see Remus and Luna, even if other supernaturals cannot?"

He remained silent for a long heartbeat. "Since they are also from the Elder Dimension, yes, I'm afraid they will. When you go into the arena to face your uncle, the other two wolves will be there, and Remus and Luna will be forced to fight them in order to protect you."

I sighed heavily and rested my elbows on my knees. I put my chin in my palms and looked at my beautiful wolves. "That's what I was afraid of."

"If you don't want that to happen, you must break the curse of the last two remaining wolves."

I scrubbed my face. "But it drains me so much."

"That was before you knew about the *Petriendo* spell."

I blinked. "Are you saying if I use the *Petriendo* spell and then the *Morphello Refulsi* spell, I won't be drained?"

He put his palm on my shoulder. "That's my theory, but you won't know for sure until you test it out."

14

Anton, Ebony, my wolves and I returned to the dining room where the others were discussing what had just happened. Someone had picked up my torn clothes and put them on an empty chair.

Ashton looked at Anton. "You knew this was going to happen, didn't you?"

Anton shrugged. "I suspected as much, but Salem had to find the right spell for it to work. This spell is one of the strongest and most powerful in the Book of Goody. She couldn't use it until she was ready."

Gloria's face brightened. "So, she's ready?"

"Almost." Anton held my gaze. "The final test will be when she faces her uncle in the arena."

"That's comforting," I mumbled.

"I put your clothes on the empty chair," Gloria said. "I didn't know what you wanted to do with them."

"I will dispose of them." Anton picked up my ruined sweater and jeans and boots. "Finish up your breakfast. You need to start on your journey soon."

I sat back down in my seat, but I wasn't sure I could eat. I smeared some cream cheese on a bagel and forced myself to take a bite.

Gloria frowned. "Are we all going to be able to fit into Ashton's SUV?"

Stefan cocked his eyebrow. "Not all of us. You don't have to worry about the three of us."

"Why not?" she asked.

"We don't need to travel by car to get to the Moon Kingdom," Julie said. "We'll move through time."

I almost choked on my bagel with excitement. "Wow, can you take us with you?" Time travel would be so cool. So much easier than we were planning.

"Unfortunately, no. You would have to be dead to use our time travel, and I don't think that's what you had in mind," Stefan said dryly.

My excitement disappeared. "Ah, no. Not at all."

Julie gave me a small smile. "I think you're forgetting that all reapers are dead."

"What's your plan?" Ashton asked.

Stefan wiped his mouth with a napkin and then stood up. "I suggest we go to Iredale Palace before the Winter Solstice and find out what's happening. We'll have to make sure we stay hidden, since I don't want to get frozen again. We will report back to you what we find."

"When?" I asked curiously.

"We will leave now and meet up with you at the overlook on Trail Ridge Road." He looked at Ashton. "That is where you plan to leave your car, isn't it?"

"Yup, that's the plan. From there, we'll head to the mountain and take the tunnel that will lead us to the Moon Kingdom." Ashton got up from the table and pulled his car keys out of his back pocket. "Is everyone almost done eating? I think Anton's right. We should get moving."

"I'm ready." I picked up my plate. "Let's just clear the table first."

"Don't worry about that," Anton said. "Cook and I will take care of the dishes. I agree with Ashton. You need to leave as soon as possible."

In less than twenty minutes, we had piled into Ashton's SUV. Anton waved to us as we pulled away, taking our usual seats—Ashton and Gloria sitting up front, Ebony and myself in the back, with Luna in between Remus and Hades acting as peacemaker. As Legacy disappeared from view, I wished again I could attend school there. I would learn so much. But apparently Legacy Academy wasn't my destiny.

None of us spoke as Ashton drove. Snow had started to fall, and the wind had picked up, making visibility difficult and forcing Ashton to drive slowly. It was as if Calvin had ordered up the storm on purpose to slow us down. Who knows, maybe he had. He could have forced Hayley to conjure a weather spell.

The SUV was nice and warm and my coat was snug. I leaned my head against the window and the rumbling SUV lulled me to sleep...

I was back in King Calvin's secret torture room. It was even colder and gloomier than I remembered. A small flickering candle that was all but melted cast long shadows on the wall.

Something moved, and I jumped.

"Don't worry, it's me. I summoned you here," a tired, weary voice croaked.

I knew that voice. "Hayley?"

"Yes." Hayley put her filthy hands on her cell's bars. Her blond hair was tangled and hopeless tears glistened in her sunken violet eyes. "Salem, he knows you're coming."

"I figured as much."

"Not to Iredale Palace. To Trail Ridge."

My eyes widened, and my heart skipped a beat. "What?"

She lowered her voice as if she were afraid any minute Calvin would burst into the torture room. "Ari and Faas are waiting for you there. You mustn't go that way."

I slid my fingers through my hair. "Then which way should we go?"

"I don't know. I don't want to know." She hung her hand. "I don't know if I could keep it from my master if I knew."

"Hayley, I can't even imagine what he's done to you." I put my hand over hers. "I promise you, someday I'll free you from this hideous place."

She lifted her head. "I hope so. I don't know how much longer I can last."

I turned and stilled. On the rack, there was blood. "Hayley..." My voice trailed off.

"Yes, he's tortured each of them. Even your aunt."

I cleared my dry throat. "Are...are they alive?"

She laughed bitterly. "They're not dead yet, no, but I must tell you, they're not in the dungeon."

I frowned. "Where are they, then?"

"They're..." Her voice trailed off and her face paled as the door to the room clicked.

"He's coming. You must go."

"Hayley, no." I grabbed the bars. "Tell me—"

She moved her hand around in a circle, and her face swam in front of me as if it was in a kaleidoscope.

I woke with a start and sat up. Beads of sweat dripped down my temples. I looked out the SUV window, searching for Ari and Faas. "Where are we?"

Ebony jumped and put a hand on her chest. "Oh, my God. You scared me."

"Where are we?" My voice rose to a panic level.

"Calm down." Ashton glanced in his rearview mirror. "We're almost at Estes Park."

I blurted, "We can't go to Trail Ridge."

Ashton gave me a you're-crazy look. "Why?" He drawled out the word.

"Because Ari and Faas will be waiting for us."

"I'm sorry?" Ashton's sarcastic voice turned super sharp.

"I had a dream about Hayley."

Gloria turned around in her seat. "My dad's witch?"

I nodded. "Yes. She told me they would be waiting there."

"Maybe you were just dreaming," Ashton said uneasily.

Gloria touched his arm. "I don't know, Ashton. Hayley is a powerful witch and she can visit you in your dreams. We were friends for a long time. We helped each other get through the dark times with my dad."

"You mean there were sunny times?" Ebony scoffed.

Gloria flashed her a scowl.

Ebony put up her hands. "Sorry. Bad joke." She turned to her gaze to Ashton. "Do you really want to chance it? Salem's dreams have been damned accurate before."

Gloria looked at each of us worriedly. "But what about the reapers? They could be walking into a trap."

"Rusty and the others can take care of themselves," Ebony said. "I wouldn't worry about them."

I wasn't quite so sure. "But what if Ari and Faas use the freezing spell on them? Last time, it froze Stefan."

"Well then, what do you want to do?"

I thought about it. "Ebony, do you think Rusty would sense them?"

She shrugged. "I don't know. I hope so."

I didn't want to tell her, but I couldn't keep it to myself. "There's something else."

Her eyes widened, and her face paled. "Is it about Gunnar? What? Tell me." Her voice screeched like a hawk.

"Not just Gunnar. Ebony, I don't think they're dead," I said. "But according to Hayley, they're not in the dungeon."

She grabbed my hand. "Then where are they?"

"I don't know, but they weren't in Calvin's secret room with Hayley, either." I looked at Gloria. "Is there someplace else your dad would take special prisoners?"

She rubbed her forehead. "Not that I know of. Although it's not like he confided in me much."

"I can't just keep driving around." Ashton turned left into downtown Estes Park. "Tell me where to go."

"Is there another town where we could drop the car that's close?" I asked.

"Nope," Ashton said flatly.

Gloria piped up, "What about Glen Haven? It's just a little bit north of here."

Ashton released a frustrated sigh. "It will be added miles that we haven't planned on."

I flashed him a teasing smile. "You said you were looking forward to a run, didn't you?"

His frown died and he slowly finally broke out in a grin. "I guess you got me there." He turned the SUV around in a parking lot and headed back out of the downtown. He turned on East Wonderview and went right past the historic Stanley Hotel that was supposed to be haunted. I'd never been there. Only watched *The Shining*.

Up close it was majestic, with its pink roof and white facade.

"You ever been there?" Ebony asked, nodding at the hotel.

I shook my head. "No, but I've always wanted to visit it. I'm a Stephen King nut and I've read all his books and watched every single one of his movies. *The Shining*'s my favorite."

"When this is all over, maybe we could all spend the weekend there," she said.

"Yeah, that would be great," I mumbled. Deep down, I wondered if this was as close as I was ever going to get to the Stanley Hotel. I hadn't really thought of what I would do if I survived the showdown with Calvin, though spending the night at the Stanley Hotel would be great, especially with Mateo at my side.

Maybe that was all wishful thinking.

Ashton climbed higher up the slick curving road and left the Stanley behind. It started snowing lightly. Glen Haven should have been a quick drive, but the icy road had deep potholes and the going was slow. The houses were becoming farther and farther apart. The snow fell harder and Ashton turned on the windshield wipers.

He turned on a curve and then the SUV hit some ice. Or at least that's what I thought it was.

Ashton swore as he grappled with the wheel, but it was as if it had a mind of its own. The SUV spun around violently, then smashed into a pine tree head on. My shoulder slammed into the door and I groaned. Pain gripped me and I gritted my teeth. The wolves yelped, and Hades snarled. I looked over and the wolves and Hades were all tangled together like a snowball.

Gloria cried out. She was holding her forehead. If she and Ashton hadn't been wearing seatbelts, they would have definitely been dead.

Ebony was panting hard.

I looked at her. "Are you all right?"

She nodded. "Just a little shaken."

Ashton turned around. "Is everyone okay?"

"Yeah," Ebony and I muttered.

He had a bump on his forehead.

"Are you all right?" I asked.

"I'm fine. Just a little bang." He opened the car door. "Stay here." He got out of the SUV and slammed the door.

"I don't think we're going anywhere." Ebony peered at her window. "And it's snowing pretty hard out there."

I scanned the outside. The sky had decided to dump so much snow that the SUV was in danger of being completely buried. "Yeah, I think that's it. We're hiking in from here to the tunnel."

Ashton whipped open the door. “We’re in deep shit.”

I went to open my door. “Why?”

He pushed my door shut again. “No, stay in the car.”

“What do you mean? We can’t do that.”

He slid into the driver’s seat. “We have to. There’s something out there.”

I peered out the window. Something dark glided through the woods. Something with silver eyes.

“Oh, shit.” I scooted back from the window.

“What is it?” Ebony asked.

I turned and looked at her. “Harpy,” I whispered.

Ashton looked at each of us. “We’re being hunted, and now we’re trapped in this damn busted-up SUV.”

Ebony pulled out her cellphone. “I’ll call Anton.” She punched in a number. “Come on, answer, answer, answer.” She slammed her phone down on her lap. “Crap, no cell service.”

Hades let out a warning snarl. I whirled around, and there was the harpy again, right outside the rear of the SUV.

Remus and Luna both growled loudly.

Two more harpies slunk out of the trees. One was on my side and another was on Ebony’s side.

We were surrounded.

15

The harpies were just as ugly as they had been the last time I saw them—women with long, straggly black hair, with their heads set on the body of an eagle. They had fearsome black wings that were plastered to their sides, but it was their silver eyes that really scared the crap out of me. The hate in them said they wanted to hurt us badly.

Then they cried out.

Shriek Shriek Shriek

It was almost as if they were announcing to someone they had found us.

"I think they're calling someone," I said, not really to anyone in particular.

"Yeah, I think you're right." Ashton shifted around uneasily in the car.

"We can't just sit here." Gloria scooted closer to Ashton as a harpy got close to her window.

"That's exactly what we're doing." Ashton put his arm around her shoulders. "One scratch for them and you're dead."

She looked wildly around the SUV as the things walked around, looking for a way inside. "Can they get in here?"

He shook his head. "I don't think so."

The harpy closest to me raised her fist and smashed on the window.

"Shit, it's going to break." I jerked toward Ebony, panting hard.

"Stay calm," Anton said. "The glass will hold. It's specially reinforced to withstand a supernatural attack."

I wasn't sure I believed him, but even though a long, ugly crack sliced along the glass diagonally, somehow the window miraculously held. But for how much longer?

Use the *Petriendo* spell, the voice of the Book of Goody whispered in my mind.

Are you kidding me? I can't fight them.

They weren't just scary looking. They were huge.

The things shrieked again.

Hades hopped into the back seat and sat between Ebony and me. She put her hand on his back. "At least it looks like whoever they're calling is taking their sweet time to come."

Fear was pumping through me something fierce. "Yeah, and by their pissed off faces, they're not happy about it."

"Well, whenever whoever is coming finally gets here, we're screwed," Ashton muttered.

Use the spell, the voice urged again. You can do this. Believe.

I leaned my head back on the seat. Anton had said the only way to know whether I was strong enough to defeat my uncle was to test my new power.

Luna leaned her head against my cheek. I petted her cheek. "Are you and Remus ready, beautiful girl?"

She licked my cheek.

Ashton whirled around in his seat. "Wait. Ready for what?"

I didn't answer him, just unzipped my jacket and wiggled out of it.

Ebony grabbed my wrist. "Salem, what are you doing?"

"Let me go."

She tightened her grip. "You're not going out there."

"Do you want to stay here and see who's coming for dinner?" My voice was surprisingly calm, even though fear was turning my spine yellower by the second.

She slowly released my wrist. "No. But are you sure you're strong enough to fight these things? They've killed some of my friends."

"I know." I ripped off my sweater and shivered. Ignoring the freezing cold air and my chattering teeth, I kicked off my boots and then stripped out of the rest of my clothes.

Ashton glared at me. "You're going to get yourself killed."

"Maybe. Maybe not." I didn't want to think about that. Anton was right—I had to know whether I could successfully use the Petriendo spell in a battle situation before I crossed my paths with my uncle.

He grabbed my arm. "Why the hell are you doing this?"

I searched his face. "Ashton, I have to face my uncle alone in the arena. He's never lost a fight. I have to find a way to defeat him if I'm going to be your queen."

He gritted his teeth. "Damn it." But he released my arm.

I looked at Ebony. "You're going to have to open a door so the demon wolves and I can get out."

She nodded and put her hand on the handle. "Are you sure you want to do this?"

A sense of calm fell over me. "Yeah, I am."

The harpies had moved away from the car and had formed a circle, as if they were waiting for me. Or had more company arrived? Either way, it was time for the show to begin.

I looked at my demon wolves and then touched the top of their heads. "*Petriendo*."

The same tingling sensations danced around my fingers, and pink sparkles flickered around my hand. Something gushed up my arm like a squirting hose. That powerful energy surged through me again. I tilted my head back.

My wolf surged forward from within me and again I shifted

faster than usual. My muscles bulked and thickened and my body grew bigger and bigger. My nails lengthened into sharp claws. I took up almost the whole back seat, squishing Hades against Ebony.

I glanced over, looking for my demon wolves, but they had turned invisible again.

Ebony shook her head. "Here goes nothing." She opened her door.

The harpies moved fast, but I was faster. I hopped out of the door and my pencil sketch demon wolves were immediately on either side of me, snarling. The harpies looked around confusedly when they heard them.

Shriek Shriek Shriek

I got the feeling the harpies were desperately calling for their master. They were scared. I could smell it. Scared out of their minds. And scared people don't always make the right decisions.

I wasn't sure if this would help or hinder me, but at least for now, the harpies couldn't see my wolves. I tilted my head at Remus. He seemed to understand and circled behind the harpies. Luna stayed where she was, and I stepped forward.

One harpy swung at me. I growled and snatched her arm, biting down and shaking it hard. Foul burning liquid rolled down my throat, almost making me gag. No matter how badly I wanted to, I refused to let go. The harpy raised her arm to strike, and that's when Luna attacked. She snatched its arm in her powerful jaw.

The other two harpies raced to help their wounded comrade, but that was their fatal error. Remus lunged and hopped onto the back of one of them, knocking them down to the ground. He bit down on her neck and shook his head. Black blood burst from her, squirting like a fountain into the air and then cascading down onto the snow.

She screamed endlessly and pounded her fists against the

ground, but he held on tight. She bucked and squirmed, trying to throw him off, but it was useless.

Slowly, she stopped moving and her body went limp as more black blood gushed out onto the ground.

The other harpy flipped out her wings and lunged into the sky, shrieking. She was definitely going to get reinforcements. We had to get the fuck out of here.

Luna and I were pulling and twisting on the third harpy's arm. Some of her blood seeped into my mouth. It burned my lips and tasted like sour wine, but I still refused to let go. She shrieked and shrieked, trying to break free, but she wasn't going anywhere.

Black blood dripping from his jaws, Remus pounced on the harpy's back, pinning her shoulders to the ground. She howled in frustration.

A car door slammed, then Ashton rushed over to us with his sword held high over his head. With a loud yell, he decapitated the harpy. Its head rolled across the snow and stopped, its lifeless eyes staring up at the sky.

Panting, I released her arm. Luna and Remus came and stood beside me.

Ashton wiped off his bloodied sword in the snow. "Damn, girl."

Gloria, Ebony, and Hades got out of the busted-up SUV. I hadn't even noticed until now just how badly it was damaged. The front end was crunched up like an accordion.

Hades slowly approached the dead harpy and sniffed cautiously. Then he bared his teeth and sat on the ground.

Ebony came up alongside him and put her hands on her hips. "You're a badass, Salem." She looked at Hades. "I think this one's mad he didn't get to join in the fun, though."

Gloria shielded her eyes with her palm. "What should we do? That thing's going to bring in the calvary."

"We need to get out of here," Ashton said. He looked at me. "Are you and your demon wolves okay? Can you travel?"

I glanced between Luna and Remus, and then back at him, and nodded. For whatever reason, the spell didn't seem to be draining them. How much power did a demon wolf possess, anyway?

Ashton went to the back of the SUV and pulled out the backpacks. "Come on, Gloria. Time to shift." He unzipped his jacket and stuffed it into his pack.

"I know. I can hardly wait to do this," Gloria grumbled as she stuffed her jacket into her pack.

She carefully took off her sweater. The wind blew her blond hair around her face and she shivered. She looked like she had come down with smallpox. She had so many goosebumps. With her teeth chattering, she quickly removed the rest of her clothing and boots, then placed them into her backpack.

She shifted into a beautiful gray wolf. The wind rustled her fur. Clearly, she wasn't freezing anymore.

Ashton was completely naked and reminded me of the Greek god Apollo. "Hades and Ebony, time to fly."

With that, he shifted into his magnificent grey wolf. I looked at my team. We were ready.

"Come on, Hades. Let's do this." Ebony nodded, and in a split second, she had changed into a huge, red-eyed bat.

She swooped down and picked up three of the backpacks in her talons. She flapped her wings and glided into the air. Even the snow didn't slow her down as her large wings sent the angry storm flying. She was magnificent.

Hades unfurled his wings, grabbed the remaining backpacks, and lunged into the air, just as fierce as Ebony.

Ashton rushed into the trees, leaping in and out of the snowbanks. Gloria, the demon wolves, and I followed him. He knew best how to get to the secret tunnel that went under the mountain that would lead us to the Moon Kingdom. I had only been there once, and didn't think I could find it on my own.

I had to force myself not to overtake Ashton, since my wolf was three times as powerful as his. I also set the pace for my wolves, who remained on either side of me. To the others, they were still invisible except for their tracks. Poor Gloria was lagging badly behind us. She was determined, and doing her best, but her wolf was slightly smaller than us, and the snowbanks practically swallowed her up.

Ashton set a quick pace. We passed trees, meadows, and homes that were bundled up against the storm as we climbed a mountain that I assumed would take us past Trail Ridge Road.

We should have stayed together. That was a mistake.

Gloria yelped.

I whirled around. She had been cut off from the rest of us by a huge black wolf that rivaled my own for size and two other gray wolves. I recognized them immediately. It was the other two demon wolves.

The one thing I didn't want to happen was about to go down. Luna and Remus were going to have to fight their siblings.

I snarled, and Luna and Remus fanned out behind me.

The black wolf turned around. It too had red eyes, but it wasn't a demon wolf. I sniffed, inhaling something foul and evil, and I shuddered.

It wasn't a wolf at all.

It was Balthazar.

"Miss me?" Velkan came up behind Gloria.

The two demons had her trapped, and they were ready to rip her apart.

16

"You fuckers aren't fighting fair, are you?"

I never was so glad to hear that angry male voice in my life. Rusty stepped out of the windy storm, his green eyes blazing.

Julie and Stefan fanned out behind Velkan and Balthazar.

Velkan glared. "Did you not learn anything, Stefan? I froze your ass last time."

Stefan smiled. "Go ahead. I won't stay that way for long."

Hades landed in front of me and snarled. I looked for Ebony, but I didn't see her. That didn't matter. She'd get here.

Velkan held up his hand. "*Silenetus*."

Snow swirled around Rusty, Julie, and Stefan, turning them into beautiful ice sculptures.

Shitshitshitshitshit

Velkan faced me and flashed me an evil smile that made me put my tail between my legs.

"Now it's your turn, princess." He pointed his finger at me. "*Silenetus*."

Snow swirled around me and I held my breath, waiting to turn into a frozen icicle. The tips of my fur frosted over—and then I sneezed.

Velkan's smile vanished. "What?"

"She's got Unseelie blood, asshole." Ebony came out of the shadows, a red, black, and gold aura surrounding her. She wasn't a bat anymore.

The demon gritted his teeth. "I know that. But Calvin is of the same bloodline, and he succumbs to the spell."

Did I hear right? Had he frozen Calvin?

"So?" Ebony held out her arms and rose into the air, hovering. "He's not the chosen one. Salem is."

"What are you?" Velkan stepped back. Was that fear in his eyes?

Ebony smiled. "You know full well. I'm mixed blood."

Velkan narrowed his eyes. "But not Unseelie." He raised his hand as if to freeze her.

I advanced on him, snarling, ready to take a bite out of his ass. Luna advanced too, ready to attack.

But we were too late.

"*Silenetus*."

Snow swirled around Ebony, dousing her aura. She began falling like a rock. Hades immediately soared into the air and swept underneath her. She landed on his back and he gently glided back into the forest. He stood guard in front of her, snarling.

Velkan grinned. "I'm going to freeze your friends one by one, princess."

Before I could do anything else, he swept his palm around, saying the spell over and over. Immediately, snow whirled around Ashton and Gloria, freezing them into ice statues. Gloria's huge, terrified eyes broke my heart.

Balthazar shifted back into his gorgeous body. "You fool, Velkan. You're about to be ripped to pieces."

Velkan frowned. "What?"

"She's drawn on the demon wolves' powers. They're invisible, and one's coming up behind you."

So, like Anton, Balthazar could see my invisible wolves, but Velkan couldn't. Interesting.

"Don't think you can keep them, girl," Balthazar warned. "I'm taking them back."

Suddenly, thunder and lightning flashed overhead. The gray clouds moved around faster and faster, as if something was coming.

Balthazar looked up. His face paled. "Damn it." He glared at me. "I'll find you soon enough, princess." He snapped his fingers and disappeared.

Just as he did so, the thunder and lightning stopped. Apparently, whatever was coming had changed its mind. We were on our own again.

One of the demon wolves snapped at Remus. Velkan looked at him in confusion. Maybe Velkan couldn't see the invisible wolves, but his wolves certainly could. The other wolf circled behind Remus. Crap, they could rip him apart. I wasn't going to let that happen.

Then Luna grabbed Velkan's thigh with her jaw.

He howled and threw his head back in pain.

Without hesitation, I shifted back into human form. Cold gripped me and I shivered, but I ignored it. All I cared about was saving Remus. I stuck out my hand to the demon wolf nearest me. "*Morphello Refulsi*."

Pink swirls swished around my fingers and then jetted out to the wolf. It lifted into the snowy sky, kicking and yelping.

"Stop it, bitch," Velkan growled. He yanked his leg away from Luna and tried to take a step toward me, but Luna slammed into his back, knocking him to the ground.

"Get off me." He struggled, putting his hands up, pushing on Luna's broad chest. He looked at the other wolf. "Help me, dammit."

The wolf charged and rammed into Luna, toppling her off Velkan, who scrambled to his feet. He had a long scratch on his face. I hadn't even seen Luna graze his skin with either of her paws, but then again, I was concentrating on what I was doing.

"Follow me." Velkan staggered into the woods with the last wolf trailing behind him.

I slowly lowered my arm and the whimpering wolf softly lowered to the ground. It shook its head and a single word popped into my mind—*Nico*. The wolf's name was Nico. He stood looking at me, as if he was still trying to clear the fog from his brain, not comprehending he was free.

Luna and Remus approached him and this seemed to spark some interest in his dazed, red eyes.

I fell to my knees, holding my arms around my waist. I desperately wanted to shift back into my wolf for warmth, but everyone around me was frozen.

Hades came out of the woods with Ebony trailing behind him.

My hair blew in my face, and I scowled. "E-e-eb-bony?" My teeth were chattering so badly I couldn't even talk.

"Hades thawed me." She plopped down next to me and put her hand on my back. "You need to shift, Salem, before you get frostbite. Hades will take care of everyone else, don't worry."

I didn't argue with her. I hoped she was right. I shifted, warmth immediately filled me, and I stopped shivering.

Hades approached Ashton first. He exhaled, and fire blazed around Ashton, melting the ice. Ashton shook himself, knocking the rest of the ice off him. The Catalan dragon stepped away from him and exhaled again. Rings of fire sailed around Gloria until chunks of ice fell from her. Like Ashton, she shimmied and the last bit of ice dropped from her tail.

Ashton immediately ran over to her and nuzzled her, comforting her.

Hades headed over to the reapers next, starting with Rusty. Ice gushed down his face. I swear his angry eyes had turned into lasers that would fry Velkan's face off the next time he saw him.

"Where is that fucker?" he snarled as he stretched his shoulders, knocking the rest of the ice off. "I'm going to kill him."

"He's gone," Ebony said. "He turned tail and ran after Salem freed the other wolf."

Rusty followed her gaze. "You're telling me we have a third wolf now on our side?"

Julie ran her fingers through her blond hair. "I think that's exactly what she's saying, Mister I'm-too-pissed-off-to-listen."

Rusty scowled at her, but then his frown faded. He gently lifted her chin. "Are you okay?" he asked softly.

I tilted my head and smiled to myself. So, the big bad boy had a soft spot for Julie.

Rusty caught me staring at him. "What the hell are you looking at?"

Julie squeezed his cheeks with her long fingers. "Will you stop? You're about to do something stupid."

"No, I'm not."

Stefan brushed the ice off his sleeve. "Rusty, I suggest you calm down so you're in control of those hot emotions of yours. I'm surprised you weren't able to burn the ice off yourself."

Rusty opened his mouth, but then shut it again. He didn't seem to want to challenge Stefan. Probably a good idea.

Julie knelt in front of Hades and rested her forearms on her knees. "Thank you for freeing us." Hades licked her face.

"Watch it," Rusty grumbled. "He isn't always nice."

Ebony rolled her eyes. "Will you please stop? That was a long time ago. You're pals now, remember?"

"Yeah. Well. If you say so." His voice was uneasy and he tightened up his grip on his scythe, as if he was afraid Hades was going to attack him.

Stefan looked at each of us. "Is your plan still to head toward the tunnel?"

As a wolf, Ashton's head nodded up and down.

"Okay. Be wary of more ambushes along the way," he said. "We don't know where Balthazar went."

Ebony frowned. "What if he went to Hell?"

Rusty gave her a teasing smile. "Then we go to Hell, too."

Dread and fear filled her eyes. "Seriously? You're going to go to Satan's funhouse?"

Julie stroked Hades' mane. "Ebony, we're reapers. We go to Hell on a regular basis to deliver souls."

Ebony shifted nervously from foot to foot. "I'm sorry. I keep forgetting that's part of your job. What if he won't let you out again?"

"Not possible." Rusty puffed out his chest and twirled his scythe, as if daring Balthazar to hold him prisoner.

Stefan cocked his eyebrow, and Rusty had the decency to turn red and look at his feet.

"Okay, Okay. He can capture reapers...but he has to catch us first."

I let out a loud bay of protest.

"I swear to you we won't get caught." He pointed his scythe at Stefan. "Besides, Father Time here is coming with us."

Stefan glared, but didn't fall into a bickering contest with him. Instead, he clasped Ebony's arm. "Be careful. We will meet up with you again in the tunnel."

She nodded. "We'll be careful."

Stefan put the tip of his scythe into the snow. "Expect anything."

Julie gave us a winning smile and moved her fingers up and down in a half wave. "Bye-bye. See you soon."

Rusty lifted his chin up high. "Later, dudes."

In a flash of light, they all disappeared.

Ebony looked down at Hades. "I hope they're careful, too." She turned to Ashton. "I take it you're ready to lead us again?"

Ashton barked and tilted his head. He nudged Gloria, who

obediently followed him. I headed over to my demon wolves. Nico lowered his head, and I nudged him, hoping he knew all was forgiven, that people or wolves couldn't be held responsible for the things they did when they were cursed.

We had to act as a team. We needed solidarity.

I tilted my head back and howled.

AAAaaaoooooo

Luna and Remus were the first to join my song. Ashton and Gloria followed next. Ebony tilted her head back and did her best imitation of a wolf howl. Hades released a loud roar.

Ebony grinned. "I guess it's no secret we're coming."

Ashton sniffed and then bolted through the trees. Gloria fell in right behind him.

Ebony changed into her bat. Once again, she and Hades grabbed our packs and flew off into the gray sky. The only good thing was the snow had lightened up. Score one point for our team.

The demon wolves and I leaped through the snow behind Ashton and Gloria. Adrenaline whipped through me. I had three demon wolves on my side now, and my uncle was down to one.

Maybe the tide was finally turning.

Look out, uncle. The Vindicators are coming and we ain't gonna take no prisoners.

17

The trek to the mountain was long and hard due to the deep snow. Sometimes it went up to our chests, even mine, and I was twice as big as the other wolves. The sun had set long ago, and we only had the stars to guide us. Somehow, though, Ashton knew exactly where we were going.

Every time I exhaled, I could see my breath. I swear I had icicles on the tips of my fur, but I didn't stop. No one did. Determination pumped through me, but my pace was getting slower and slower. My muscles ached and screamed for me to stop, but I didn't give into their complaints.

I wasn't the only one struggling. Gloria had retreated to the rear, but Nico stayed with her. No one was going to be left behind.

We just kept moving. Ashton set a brutal pace, not even letting us stop for food, but it was probably for the best. Shelter was our number one concern, and the tunnel would protect us from the plummeting temperatures.

My wolf was getting beyond weary. My belly was empty and my poor paws were frozen. I hoped that once we were inside the tunnel, we could light a fire. The only good thing was that my thick fur kept me warm from the cruel wind.

So far we hadn't been attacked, but I had a sinking feeling it would happen when we reached the tunnel or, worse, were inside it.

Hades and Ebony swirled around us overhead, and they never made a warning cry that they had seen the enemy. That was good.

I had only been here once before, but a stream with a beaver pond was jogging my memory. Other things started to look familiar, too—a twisted pine that was almost completely bent over, a grove of aspens with a huge rock in the middle of them, a deep ravine. We were getting closer.

Finally, Ashton slowed and sniffed around a cliff. He shifted into human form, pressed on a rock, and said something that I couldn't hear over the blowing wind.

Ebony and Hades landed next to us. I looked around, but there was no sign of the reapers. I hoped Balthazar didn't have them locked up in some torture chamber.

Ashton said something in a louder voice, but I still couldn't understand him. He pushed and pushed, his massive shoulders straining, and finally the rocky side of the mountain moved as if by magic. Snow burst inside. He stepped into the darkness and we all slipped in behind him.

"*Defenum,*" he whispered.

The great door creaked back into place, leaving us in utter darkness. I strained to hear anything, but all I could hear was the wind howling angrily outside in protest that it hadn't been invited inside.

"Hades, make some fire," Ebony whispered. "We need to see where we are."

The Catalan dragon exhaled a puff of fire, lighting up the cave for a few moments. The tunnel seemed to go on forever.

Ebony picked up a rock and put it near us. "Hades, can you please heat the rock?"

He exhaled until the rock glowed red, warming the area around us.

Gloria shifted and quickly put on her black leggings, a thick black sweater, and her boots. She rubbed her hands over the rock. "Oh, this feels so good. I'm still freezing. Even my wolf was succumbing to the cold."

I shifted back to a human. "*Transes*."

Ebony looked at Remus and Luna and smiled. "I almost thought they had left us."

Ashton shifted back into his human form and grabbed his backpack. "Why didn't you keep them hidden?"

I pulled on my jeans. "Because I thought I should save the spell for when we really needed it. I'm not sure what it's going to do to them. I only want to use it when I face pure evil."

"Good point," he said.

Nico and Remus curled up next to Luna, who was already sleeping quietly. They were all exhausted and, I'm sure, hungry. As was I.

I wiggled into my thick sweater and then zipped up my coat. "What did Anton's cook pack for us? We're all hungry, including Hades and the wolves."

Ashton unzipped a backpack. "Let's see what we have." He pulled out several bags carefully wrapped in white cloth that I had a feeling kept the food fresher than any plastic or foil made in the human world.

I unwrapped the first cloth and smiled. Raw steak. I looked over at my wolves, who all stared at the meat with their tongues hanging out. I laughed. "Relax, there's enough for all of you."

I got up and gave Hades one, and then one to each of the wolves.

Ashton rubbed his chin. "How did Anton know we would have an extra wolf?"

I shrugged. "I don't know."

"Because he believes in you," Ebony said softly. "And I bet if you look closer, there is one more for the last wolf."

I didn't answer her. Sometimes all this faith in me was overwhelming. I was getting stronger, but the final test was coming up, and I honestly didn't know if I had what it would take to free Mateo and the others, and defeat my uncle.

Ashton opened several more of the cloths and put the huge chicken sandwiches on the red-hot stone. The sandwiches were definitely fit for a king. I inhaled the smell of chicken and my stomach growled loudly. "Here, have some cheese and nuts."

He gave each of us several cheese sticks that we all devoured. He then handed us smaller sacks that were filled with walnuts, almonds, macadamia nuts, and cashews. Once the sandwiches were heated, I bit into mine and realized that it had cheddar cheese and pickles as well. I swear it was the best chicken sandwich I had ever eaten.

Gloria yawned. "I'm sorry."

I chuckled. "Don't be." I stretched my arms wide and yawned, too. "You're not the only one. I think we need to get some much-needed sleep."

"You rest," Ashton said. "I'll stand guard first."

"Wake me when you can't keep your eyes open."

He nodded. "Fair enough."

I curled up next to my wolves and laid my head on Remus' soft side. Their snores lulled me to sleep, and for once, I dreamed of nothing, not even Mateo.

Someone shook me hard. "Salem, wake up. It's morning." Ashton yawned. "Time to get going."

I sat up, rubbing my eyes. "Did you get any sleep at all?"

His eyes were bloodshot. "I dozed off and on. You need your rest."

I clasped his arm. "So do you. You don't have always to take care of us."

"I know, but I want to. It's my job."

I wanted to argue with him, but knew it would be pointless. Hades' heated rock had returned to its normal color, and the cold had slipped its freezing fingers into the cave. I shivered. Some daylight was streaming into the cave, but it wasn't much. The further we went down the tunnel, the darker it would become.

"Cook also sent us a cold breakfast," Ashton said. "Sliced cheese, hard boiled eggs, and cold bacon. He sent some raw hamburger too for Hades and the wolves. Anton thinks of everything."

"He is amazing," I said. "You're so lucky you got to attend Legacy." I took a big bite of my cold bacon. "That's something I'll never get to do."

"But you'll be a queen."

I gave some of my bacon to Luna, who was lying right next to me. Hades, Remus, and Nico were staring fixedly down the tunnel. I had an uneasy feeling about that. All I could see was darkness, but they must have seen something I couldn't.

Ashton followed my gaze. "Can you sense what they sense?"

I shook my head. "No. Not as a human."

"Do you think you should borrow power from them and shift into your wolf?"

"Not yet. Like I said, I want to do that when it's absolutely necessary."

Ashton stood up and lugged his backpack over his shoulder. "Got it. Well, time to go."

Gloria gripped the strap of her backpack tightly. "It's so dark."

"It's going to get darker." Ashton headed over to Hades. "Pretty soon you won't be able to see your hand in front of your face, and the tunnel gets narrower and narrower."

"I remember," I said. "Not looking forward to it."

"Shouldn't we use some kind of light just to see where we're going?" Gloria said.

Ashton glanced over his shoulder. "No. It was bad enough that we had Hades heat up the stone till it glowed. There could be something down there waiting for us."

"That's why we should use a light," she protested.

Ashton turned and faced her. "Gloria, if someone is in the cave with us, they already know we're here."

Her face paled, and she bit her lip.

"Gee, that's comforting." Ebony tossed her bag over her shoulder. "Okay, let's get this over with."

Ashton stepped in front of Hades and my wolves. "Let me go first."

I held up my hand. "Wait. Do you really think something's waiting down there for us?"

He exhaled slowly. "Yeah, I do. Twice last night I thought I saw an orange light, but then it quickly went out. I wasn't sure if it was my imagination or if something was there."

I stared at my three wolves. "Nico, Luna, Remus." They looked over to me. "Ready for the *Petriendo* Spell?"

Nico looked at me curiously, but Remus and Luna wagged their tails.

"So *now* you're going to use it?" Ashton's eyebrow quirked as if to tell me I was being wishy-washy with the use of the spell.

"You didn't mention earlier that you saw a light. It could be Faas."

He looked back down the tunnel and then scowled. "My sentiments exactly."

It made me feel like a teenage girl, always changing her outfits just to impress some dumb guy, but I quickly took everything off again and then placed it all in my backpack.

Ashton bent down and picked it up.

"Thank you." I put my hands on Remus' and Nico's heads and laid my cheek on Luna's back. "*Petriendo*."

I arched my back as the demon wolves' power rushed through me, strengthening me and making me bigger and bulkier. I quickly shifted into my wolf and I realized I was much bigger than any of them.

"It's so weird that the wolves disappear," Gloria said.

I looked back at Ashton, Ebony, Hades, and Gloria. This was our final trek before we reached Iredale Palace, and I didn't want to lose any of them. I had to protect them.

Ashton went to get in front of my wolves and me, but I immediately nudged him out of the way, refusing to let him pass.

He glared and swiped my tail. "Salem, what are you doing? I'm supposed to lead."

Protecting your ass. What do you think?

Remus led us down the tunnel, and just as Ashton had said, the walls began to close in and darkness fell over us.

But then something happened that I didn't expect.

My heart quickened. I could see in the dark. I had never been able to do that before. Was it because I had added Nico? Were there other things I could do now as well?

Our footsteps padded softly down the tunnel as we kept going deeper and deeper into the darkness. Shadows danced at the edges of the tunnel. Even with my new eyes, I couldn't tell if there was something there, or if my eyes were playing tricks on me.

But then I caught a scent.

Something metallic.

Blood.

18

My hackles stood straight up and I snarled. Remus, Nico, and Luna growled and flattened their ears way back.

Hades released a low roar behind me. He must have sensed the blood, too.

But it wasn't just blood.

There was a wild fear.

The walls were too narrow for me to move past my wolves. We had no choice but to go forward. There was no retreat.

Remus slowly crept on. I could see over his head, but couldn't make out the shadows moving about. They were at least five or six of them.

Hummp Humpf Humpf

What was that? With every step we took, the muffled sound got louder and louder, the smell of blood stronger and stronger.

Cool air rushed over me and I realized that the walls of the tunnel had widened.

Suddenly, the lanterns hanging in the tunnel turned on, giving off a soft glow. I hissed at what I saw.

A blond, blue-eyed woman was smiling at me. Her hair was

almost down to her elbows. She stood with her legs shoulder width apart. "Well, well, well." She clapped. "I finally get to meet the missing wolf princess." She put her palm on her chest. "I was a princess once, too. I'm Kara."

Gunnar's sister? I had heard of her. She had the ability to read minds, even compel people to do things against their will.

She ran an appraising look over me and pulled out her sword. "Hmm…you are a gigantic wolf. I can see why Calvin fears you."

Seriously? Calvin was afraid of me?

Her brows furrowed. "Strange. For some reason, I can't read your mind. Using some powerful mojo, are you?"

Interesting. Somehow, being in wolf form protected me from her magic. Or was it my Unseelie blood?

She looked behind me. "Where are your demon wolves? All I see is the rubble."

Remus, Luna, and Nico were fanned out in front of her. Even more interesting.

Right in front of you, bitch.

She tapped her sword on her palm. "Calvin is going to be *so* disappointed." She stepped back and fear flashed in her eyes as she scanned the space in front of her. "Wait. Are the wolves here? Are they invisible?"

Ashton laughed. "I wouldn't make any sudden moves if I were you."

"Because I have something I propose to trade with you in exchange for the wolves."

I didn't like the sound of that.

Ashton gritted his teeth. "What?"

Kara looked over her shoulder. "Bring him in, boys."

Hmmmf Hmmmf Hmmmf

Two burly men dragged Gunnar out of the darkness, each holding an arm. He was half naked and gagged. His white hair was tangled. Ugly black and blue welts and red lash marks covered every inch of his body.

I growled and pulled back my upper lip. Tears welled in my eyes and my heart broke for him. If he looked like that, what had happened to Mateo?

"No," Ebony wailed behind us. Her dragon horns shot out of her head.

Ashton drew his sword. "How could you do that to him? He's your brother."

Kara's eyes widened. "Me? I didn't do this. This is all Calvin."

"But why?" Ebony's voice was strained.

"Why, Your Majesty?" Her mocking tone made my hackles bristle. The bitch was pushing her luck.

Kara pinched her brother's cheek roughly. "Because the idiot wouldn't form an alliance with him, that's why."

"And you would?" Ashton sneered.

Kara glared. "I'd do anything, and I mean anything, to get out of the Hollows."

Ashton brushed past me with his sword drawn. "Even sell your soul to the devil?"

"You don't know what it's like there." Her voice cracked and a flash of agony glistened in her eyes.

I almost felt sorry for her.

Almost.

"But I do." Rusty, holding his scythe, appeared with a flash on the other side of her.

Kara jerked away from him. "Stay away from me." She whirled around. "Where's Stefan?"

Rusty shrugged. "Meeting with the big bosses. They're having a special pow-wow all about you."

She licked her lips nervously. "Why?"

"Dunno. I wasn't invited." Rusty stepped toward her and narrowed his eyes. "You've been a naughty, naught, *naughty* stuck-up bitch. Someone wants to see you and your ape-man back behind bars."

"I'll freeze you if you come any further."

"Sorry, Sweet Cakes," Rusty said. "I've got new armor. Your freezing stunt won't work on me."

"You're lying," she spat. She held out her palm. "*Silenetus*."

Snow swirled around Rusty, but he just flicked a snowflake with his fingers. "See? New badge of honor, bitch."

She edged closer to a tall, bulky, dark-haired guy with cool, pearly-green eyes. "How can this be?"

Rusty shrugged. "Believe it or not, I can thank the Archangel Michael. For once in his life, he wasn't a prick."

Julie flashed next to Rusty and glared. "You shouldn't call him that, or he's going to lift the armor right back off your butt." She held her scythe in one hand. "Kara, wow...I see you've been hanging out with the wrong crowd again."

The dark-haired goon stepped in front of Kara protectively. "Stay away from her."

Rusty cocked his eyebrow. "Or what, Killian? You're going back to Funkytown, too."

Killian narrowed his eyes. "We didn't ask to be let out."

"No, you didn't." Julie agreed. "But you didn't decline the offer either."

"Oh, what? You thought we'd say no? We don't want to stay and rot in the Hollows, you stupid bitch."

Julie gasped.

Rusty lunged and put the tip of his scythe under Killian's chin, forcing him to tilt his head back. "Never talk to her like that again. Apologize right now or die."

"No, please don't hurt him." Kara raced around and clasped Killian's arm.

Rusty didn't look at her. His gaze was on Killian. "Tell him to apologize."

Kara shook his arm. "Killian, say you're sorry. Please."

Killian bit his lip and stubbornly stared at Rusty, who pushed the scythe deeper. Blood trickled down Killian's neck.

"Killian..." Kara pleaded.

Killian gritted his teeth. "Sorry." Like anyone believed him.

Rusty dug the scythe even deeper into his flesh. More blood slipped down his throat. "Say it like you mean it."

"Please," Kara begged as she pulled on his arm.

Killian stole a sideways glance at Kara, then looked at Julie and sighed heavily. "I'm sorry I spoke to you like that."

"I don't—"

Julie slapped Rusty's arm. "Enough is enough. He apologized. Now leave it be."

"You're lucky she's here," Rusty said as he slowly lowered his scythe.

Killian rushed him, but he didn't get very far. Nico charged and bit into his arm, pulling him down. Blood spurted all over his shirt and onto the ground. He pushed on Nico's head feebly. "What is this? I can feel something but not see it. Let go of me."

Ashton flashed him a smirk. "Invisible demon wolf. Just to warn you, they're all around you. If you make one false move, the rest of them will attack."

Kara turned an anguished gaze on me. "You can control them, Salem. Tell them to stop."

I didn't trust her as far as I could throw her, but it was time to up the ante. I shifted back and could care less if I was naked. Cold seized me and I shivered.

Ashton handed me his jacket. "Here. Put this on."

I slipped into Ashton's warm wool jacket that hit me mid-thigh.

"Nico, release him," I commanded.

The wolf slowly let go of Killian's arm and the Unseelie edged away.

"Now, Kara, free Gunnar, or I'll tell them to rip your precious Killian apart."

I had just learned something. I didn't always have to change into a wolf. My wolves would stay invisible even if I was in human form.

"I can't," Kara said miserably. "Calvin promises he'll have me and Killian killed if we double-cross him."

"And the demon wolves will kill you and Killian if you don't. Your choice."

Boom Boom Boom Boom

I glanced into the darkness. Heavy footsteps were pounding on the ground. It sounded like an army.

"There are guards coming up behind us." Gloria's voice trembled with fear.

"That's right, princess. Your dad isn't very happy with you." Kara grinned scornfully. "Did you really think I came here without backup?"

"Your father is very, very, very disappointed in you, Gloria," an evil voice said. I recognized it. I turned around. It was Bill, the foul guard that had been with Velkan capturing the eagles. He had a blade at Gloria's throat.

Ashton lifted his sword. "Let her go."

Bill narrowed his eyes. "You wish. She's been a naughty girl and deserves to be punished."

Nico growled and pulled back his upper lip. He squeezed through us, pressing Ashton into the wall. I had a feeling Bill hadn't been too nice to Nico, a decision he would learn to regret.

"Release her and you won't get hurt," I said.

Bill chuckled. "Nice try, princess. But your game—"

He cried out as he lurched into the wall, blood splattering from his thigh, and a look of pain spread across his sneering face. His eyes fluttered shut, and he dropped to the ground like a stone. He released his grip on Gloria. Ashton immediately snatched her by the wrist and tossed her behind him.

"Stay away from her." He brandished his sword at the other astonished guards who were staring at Bill as if he'd been attacked by a ghost.

"If you don't want to suffer the same fate as him, I suggest you leave," I said.

Nico scratched the ground with his paws, leaving eight long scratches.

"Let's get out of here," the guard nearest Bill said.

The other two didn't argue, and all three spineless jellyfish ran to the back of the cave.

I smiled. "Good boy."

Nico quickly joined his siblings.

Guards crowded us from behind and more streamed out of the tunnel.

Kara opened and shut her mouth like a goldfish. Fear was creeping into her blue eyes, but Killian wasn't so easily intimidated.

He rubbed the blood from his throat. "You're going to pay for this, reaper."

Rusty squared off with him. "Bring it on, dick."

Wow, Killian definitely had a death wish. Rusty wasn't someone I wanted to tangle with in a dark alley.

Gunnar twisted his head from side to side and mumbled something under his gag. But I couldn't make out the words. His eyes seemed to be focused on Ebony.

Ebony nodded as if she understood and then put her hand on Hades' mane. "Hades, go to Gunnar."

Hades unfurled his wings, nearly knocking Gloria and Ebony down.

Kara looked at the guards, who had just rushed into the cave. "You idiots, don't let Hades approach Gunnar."

I glanced at Ebony. "Why?"

"Hades is part of Gunnar, like a magical tattoo. They're one. It's Unseelie magic."

The three guards drew their swords and fanned out in front of Gunnar.

"Attack," I said softly.

A discordant symphony of growls and snarls instantly filled the room. Three guards immediately fell on their back. Deep claws marks appeared on their legs. They screamed in agony, but I didn't care.

"Damn," Rusty muttered. "We're going to be busy tonight."

Killian's face paled. "Shit," he murmured.

Hades didn't hesitate. He flew straight toward Gunnar.

"No," Kara howled, but her protest fell on deaf ears. She tried to block Hades, but tripped over one guard tussling with Luna and went down like a sack of hammers.

Hades smashed into Gunnar's naked chest and for a moment, it looked like he had disappeared entirely. But then a tattoo appeared on Gunnar's chest in which Hades' wings were stretched out wide and he had a snarl on his face. Gunnar arched his back and my eyes widened. The purple and blue bruises and the bloody slashes on Gunnar's battered body faded.

He yanked free of the two guards holding him while they were mesmerized by the sound of the screams and the sight of the blood spewing at their feet.

The other guards stopped struggling and lay on the floor in a bloody heap. Kara scrambled up. Her white coat was now stained red.

I patted my naked thigh. "Nico, Remus, Luna, come."

My wolves obeyed and left the guards sprawled out on the floor, moaning. They were lucky they weren't dead.

Killian, Kara, and the rest of the guards edged away from the fallen guards and looked at me.

"Are they with you?" Kara whispered.

I cocked my eyebrow. "For now."

The guards behind Killian and Kara looked at each other and then turned tail and ran back down into the dark tunnel.

Gunnar ripped the gag out of his mouth and rested his head against the wall. "Finally." Panting, he looked at Kara. "You shouldn't have sided with Calvin."

"I didn't have a choice and you know it," she hissed.

Stefan flashed in front of Kara and Killian. "I find that hard to believe."

"Don't take us back there, please." She backed up into the guards, who were grumbling behind her.

Stefan looked at Gunnar. "What do you wish me to do, Sire?"

Gunnar scrubbed his face. "As much as I hate to do this, they need to return—"

"No. No. *No.*" Kara stamped her feet and clenched her fists. "How could you do this to me? I'm your sister."

Gunnar blinked and then laughed. "It's different when the shoe's on the other foot, isn't it?"

She clamped her mouth shut.

"Stefan, I believe both she and Killian need to attend your academy," Gunnar said.

"I refuse to go to a damn school," Killian growled.

"Then you'll never get out of The Hollows," Stefan said simply. "You're lucky I'm even considering the king's proposal—"

Killian scoffed. "King? Puh-leeease."

Stefan grabbed Killian by the throat and lifted him six inches off the ground. "I suggest you learn some manners."

Killian's face turned purple, and he slapped weakly at Stefan's hand.

"Stop. You're hurting him."

Stefan completely ignored Kara and shook Killian harder. "I am done with both of your antics. You and your little Miss over here continue to align yourself with scum. I suggest you change your tune, or I'll throw you into the dungeon and you'll never see the light of day again."

He released Killian abruptly, who fell to his knees, gasping for breath.

"Do we understand each other?" His pissed-off tone left little doubt that if Killian wanted to survive at the Hollows, there was only one answer.

Killian looked up with pure hatred in his eyes, but he spat out a yes. Or at least I thought it was a yes. Kara knelt next to him and wiped his face with her sleeve.

"How long will we have to stay in your stu—I mean, your academy?" She glanced nervously up at Stefan.

He gave her a deadpan smile. "You know the rules. Until you both repent. And from what I can see, that's going to be a long, long time."

Rusty came up alongside Killian and Julie on the other side of Kara.

Stefan looked at me. "Our part in this scuffle has ended. The archangels specifically said you must win this battle alone. We can no longer interfere. Good luck to you."

Rusty frowned and shook his head. "Dicks."

Julie glared. "Do you have a death wish or something? Stop."

Rusty sighed and stared at her. "Only for you, beautiful."

"I'm going to be sick," Killian muttered.

Rusty slapped him hard on the back of the head. "Shut up. Or I'll stuff this scythe right up your ass."

"Stefan, wait," I said. "What about Balthazar?"

He gave me a tight smile. "Sorry. Like I said. We can't interfere."

With that, he snapped his fingers, and Kara, Killian, and the reapers all disappeared.

Along with the answer to my question.

19

Ebony brushed past me, nearly tripping over the wolves, and jumped into Gunnar's open arms.

"I thought…I thought I lost you," she said as she planted kisses all over his face.

He threaded his fingers through her hair. "You nearly did."

Gloria leaned close to me. "Would you like to get dressed?" she whispered.

I turned away. "Yeah, I would."

She handed me my backpack, and I quickly threw on my sweater, jeans, and boots again.

I looked at my wolves. "*Transes*."

The power in me subsided and Nico, Remus, and Luna all reappeared.

Gunnar set Ebony down on her feet and held her hand. "Whoa. What just happened? Where did those demon wolves come from?"

"It's a spell," I said. "I'm connected with them. Long story." I finished pulling on my boots. "Gunnar, what's going on with the others?"

"Nothing good," he mumbled.

That wasn't what I wanted to hear.

Don't cry Don't cry Don't cry

I took a deep breath. "Please tell me about Mateo."

He sighed and tilted his head. "He's waiting for you outside the tunnel."

I brightened up, but then the look on his face crushed my hopes. "He's not alone, is he?"

"Faas and Ari are with him."

I slapped my thigh. "Shit."

Ashton looked at me curiously. "You didn't think you would be able to just walk into the Moon Kingdom, did you?"

"Well, no..."

He cocked his eyebrow.

"But come on!" I threw up my hands. "We fought off harpies, Kara and Killian, and their goons. Now we have to fight Ari and Faas too. When is this going to end?"

Gunnar smiled grimly. "When you're queen."

"You mean if I become queen." I stroked the top of Nico's head. He had blood on and around his muzzle. Of the three wolves, he was the most aggressive.

Each of them had their own personalities. I loved them all.

"Are there any other surprises we should know about?" Ashton asked.

An idea popped into my brain. "Gunnar, do you know where the Rose Box is?"

"Yeah, I do. You're not going to like it, though." His grim voice only added to the weight already bearing down on my shoulders.

"Spit it out." I folded my arms, dreading the answer.

"It's in the first King's mausoleum, and the kicker is, Calvin forced Hayley to create a spell making it so that only you can enter."

"That's not so bad," Gloria said.

He held my gaze. "And the minute you walk inside, Balthazar will appear."

"Great. Just great. I can't fight Balthazar. The only thing he's afraid of is the Archangel Michael, and according to the reapers, they only get involved if they deem it important enough."

Gloria frowned. "Well, how do you know they won't think that's important? Maybe they will."

I looked at Gloria and wanted to give her a smart retort, but she was only trying to help and right now, I needed a bit of positivity to get me out of my woe-is-me dumps.

Ashton peered down the dark tunnel. "I can't see anything down there. Doesn't mean we're not going to be ambushed again, though. If they're not in the tunnel, they sure as hell will be waiting outside."

Luna came up alongside him and sat down. She sniffed, but didn't react.

"How many should we be expecting?" I asked.

Gunnar laughed bitterly. "Oh, you know. Just the guards that you scared the crap out of, and Ari and Faas. Those two alone could easily kick our ass."

Ebony kissed his cheek. "But you're forgetting one thing—Ari's scared shitless of Hades."

My eyes brightened. "He is? That's great. Is Faas afraid of him, too?"

"No." She sighed. "That bastard isn't afraid of anything."

I ran my hand down Nico's back. "What about invisible demon wolves?"

She shrugged. "I don't know. But I'm sure those guards are telling Ari and Faas about what happened in here. I don't think you can count on a sneak attack."

I ran my fingers through my hair. "You're probably right."

"We have to do something." Ashton looked at each of us in turn. "We can't stay here."

"Maybe we should." Gunnar rubbed his chin.

We all blurted at once. "What?"

"Look," he said. "There's a raging storm outside. Even Ari and Faas are probably freezing their asses off."

"But I thought Faas could throw fireballs," I said.

"Deadly fireballs," Ebony said. "Faas has killed more than one of our friends with them."

"He can—agreed. But he can't stop the blowing wind or the falling snow. Eventually, they are going to have to seek shelter." Gunnar's voice was rising with excitement and his eyes were shifting back and forth as he thought.

I thought I knew where he was going with this. "Are you saying we should set a trap?"

Ebony looked dubious. "Trap Ari and Faas? We needed an army last time to beat them. For all we know, the harpies are with them."

I held up a finger. "But we've already killed two."

"You mean you and the demon wolves," Ashton corrected me.

Gunnar gave me an appreciative gaze. "Really? That's impressive. Maybe trapping Ari and Faas isn't totally out of the question."

"Do you think that they'll bring Mateo with them?" I asked. I wasn't sure. If those two were seeking warm shelter, I doubted that Mateo was included.

"I don't know," Gunnar said. "They're not known for their generosity. My guess would be they'd leave him to freeze to death. You're the one they want. He's just bait."

This was becoming way too confusing. "What are they planning to do with me? Take me to my uncle?"

"No," he stated flatly. "Kill you."

I gasped and stilled. "Are you kidding? I thought Calvin wanted to face me in the arena and have a death match."

Gunnar drew a deep breath and exhaled with a curse. "Calvin wants you dead, Salem. You're a threat to him, and he wants you out of the way."

"In a fair fight," I countered.

Gunnar gave me a you're-fooling-yourself look but didn't argue with me.

Gloria gently touched my shoulder. "Salem, when has my father ever fought fair?"

I scowled. "What do you mean?"

"He wanted to be king, but he didn't challenge your father in a fair fight. He poisoned him. And he didn't even do that himself. He forced a witch to do it for him."

"But I thought he had to fight me in order for the other wolf kingdoms to accept him as king."

She gripped my shoulders and squeezed gently. "If you're dead, then they don't have any other choice but to accept him, do they?"

I studied her, trying to decide whether she'd gone off the deep end. Her father couldn't be that big of a coward, could he? Then I looked at each of my team and realized I was the delusional one.

I scrubbed my face. "Great. I can't believe this."

"He's calling in all his markers." Gunnar's gaze was fixed on me as if trying to get me to accept the cold, hard facts. "Balthazar, Kara, Killian, and now Faas and Ari."

"Okay," I said. "So what's the plan?"

He gestured toward my wolves. "Can you make them invisible again?"

"Of course. And then?"

He put his hand to his chest. "Then I think it's time for Hades to rejoin us."

Ebony clasped his elbow. "Are you sure you're healed enough?"

He kissed her softly on the lips. "Yes. Believe in me."

She wound her arms around his neck and kissed him. He crushed her against his chest.

The rest of us looked away, giving them a much-needed moment. Their embrace made me want to run down the tunnel to rescue Mateo, but that's exactly what those two assholes were expecting.

I had to stay cool, or we'd both end up dead.

Ashton cleared his throat. "Um, guys?"

Ebony and Gunnar groaned, but they ended their kiss.

She stared into his eyes. "Just for the record—I have always believed in you. So, tell me, my King of the Dark Demons, what is your plan?"

"Well, to get them to come inside we need live bait—"

Ebony put a hand on his chest. "You don't mean you, do you?"

He didn't look at me and just kept staring into Ebony's troubled eyes. "Yes."

As much as I didn't want to say it, I murmured quietly, "But it's not you they really want, is it?"

"You can't go out there." Ashton's haughty tone only made me want to do it even more, just to prove that I could.

"I won't be going out there alone, Ashton."

Gunnar clapped his shoulder. "And dude, she and her wolves already killed two harpies."

Ashton sighed heavily. "I know. But this is Ari and Faas we're talking about. The demon wolves may be invisible, but if Faas gets a fireball off at one of them, I don't know if they could survive."

I thought about it for a minute. "Then we need a distraction."

"What kind of distraction?" Ashton asked uneasily.

I looked at all of them. "What if we had someone come up behind them?"

"Who?" Ashton asked suspiciously. "It would take too long for any of us to climb the mountain, especially in this weather."

I didn't look at him and stared at Gunnar. He wasn't going to like this. "I was thinking Hades and Ebony."

"Hell no," Gunner snapped. "Not happening."

Ebony gently put her fingers on his rigid jaw and turned him to face her. "So, you were willing to risk your life to save us, but you won't let me do the same?"

"That's different." A thunder cloud settled over his face as if the matter was settled.

"It's not."

He jerked his chin away like a stubborn donkey. "Yes, it is. You're my queen."

She stood in front of him and ran her finger down his temple. "And you're my king."

"This is ridiculous. Why you?"

She kissed him on the mouth briefly. "Isn't it obvious? Because I can fly."

"So can I."

"But they need you in here. Ashton can't fight them alone. Hades won't let anything happen to me, you know that."

"And they'll be drawn to you as well, Gunnar," I said. "I know it sucks, but I don't think we have any other choice."

Gunnar clenched his fists and whirled around. "Damn it." He looked at me. "She's my mate."

I stiffened. "Yes. And mine's out there freezing to death."

He lowered his head. "I know. I'm sorry. Okay…I guess Hades and Ebony will go behind them in case they try to retreat, and hopefully they can free Mateo, but what are we going to do?"

"We need to draw them into the cave," I said. "So Gunnar and I will open the door, and when we see them, we pretend to panic and don't close the door again all the way. They'll be able to come in."

Gunnar snorted. "Do you really believe they'll think we're that dumb?"

"I don't know," I said miserably. "Maybe if they're freezing their asses off, they won't care?"

Gloria couldn't hide the fear in her eyes. "Once we get them in here, then what are we going to do?"

I shrugged and tried to sound brave. "Then it's up to me and the demon wolves."

Ashton folded his arms across his chest. "To do what, exactly?"

I exhaled a harsh breath. "I don't know." My frustration was getting the best of me and his constant questions irritated me, especially since I didn't know the answer. "Wound them badly enough for us to get out of here? Maybe Stefan could come and collect them?"

"He said he wouldn't be able to help."

Ashton's negativity was about to send me over the edge.

"Do you have a better plan?" I couldn't keep the irritation out of my voice.

"No. I don't. But I have the distinct feeling that not all of us will survive this endeavor."

Some of the anger melted away from me and my shoulders sagged. I was the leader in this mess. Suddenly, I knew what it felt like to be a general and send men into battle, knowing that some would die.

Could I really do this?

Gunnar gave me a sympathetic look. "I know this isn't easy, Salem. But we all knew the dangers when we signed up for this task. Calvin and his minions haven't given us any choice."

Ashton slammed the hilt of his sword against his chest. "I have always sworn to protect you, Princess, and I will do so now."

Gloria stood taller. "King Calvin may be my dad, but he's never been a proper father to me. I want to serve a queen that will show mercy and bring peace back to my people. I will fight by your side too, Salem."

Gunnar bowed slightly. "I have already pledged my life, my queen, and my kingdom to you. I will follow you to the end."

Ebony clasped my hand and spoke rapidly. "And I'm following you because you're my friend and that's what friends do."

My wolves all nudged me with their wet noses. Tears escaped my eyes and splashed down my cheeks. I wanted to thank them, but a lump of joy and humbleness clogged my throat. Never had I ever expected to have such loyal friends.

Words were lost to me for several long, deep breaths. Fear of vulnerability had led me to bottle up my feelings, and that had cost me dearly. I regretted not telling Mateo I loved him before

Calvin practically snatched him right out of my arms. I wouldn't make the same mistake again

I cleared my throat. "Growing up in foster care, life was hard. Friends were difficult to come by. I never knew what it was like to have a family where people were willing to stand by you until the very end. Until now." More tears fell, but I wasn't ashamed of them this time. "Thank you."

We stepped closer to each other, even the wolves, bowing our heads and putting our arms around each other, knowing this was it.

Some of us might not make it.

But if we didn't fight Calvin, innocent lives would be lost...and those lives were worth fighting for.

20

We stepped away from our embrace and looked at each other. Go Time.

"How far to the end of the tunnel?" I asked.

"I suspect we are only halfway through," Ashton said. "We should start now."

Gunnar shook his head. "No. We're all drained. We need to sleep, even for a couple of hours."

"But we could be ambushed…" Ashton countered.

"I know you're worried, Ashton." Gunnar clasped his friend's shoulder. "But do you really want to face Faas and Ari with your ass dragging?"

Ashton's shoulders sagged. "No, I don't. Okay, I'll stand the first watch."

Gunnar dropped his arm. "So be it. Wake me in a couple of hours."

I wanted to volunteer, but after fighting the harpies and facing down Kara and Killian, my body was weary. "Thank you for doing this."

The two guys nodded.

Gunnar clasped Ebony's hand. "We'll be, um, down the

tunnel." He didn't have to say what they were going to do. I could see the passion brewing in his and Ebony's eyes. I only wished it was me and Mateo that were sneaking off for some sexy times.

I stretched out on the cold ground and my wolves immediately curled up around me. Their fur was warm and soft. I had barely nuzzled up to Luna when sleep overtook me…

The wind was howling, and I was stumbling around in deep snow. Once again, I was alone, with no idea where my team had gone. A blizzard blinded my vision and I could barely see two feet in front of me. My teeth were chattering and my coat couldn't keep the cold from getting into my shaking bones. I thought about shifting into my wolf, but then, in the distance, I saw what looked like a campfire.

I slowly made my way through the pines, their branches heavy with wet snow.

I froze. That wasn't any campfire.

A tall, blond man stood next to a boulder, nonchalantly tossing a fireball up and down in his palm. With his beard and mustache, he reminded me of a mountain man. That had to be Faas.

"Will you hurry up and warm up the damn boulder?" an evil voice hissed.

The voice was so terrifying it made the wind colder around me. I wanted to run and hide, but for better or worse, I was drawn to the two of them. I darted behind a tree.

Another blond man was squatting on the ground with his arms wrapped around his knees.

Faas laughed. "Freezing, Ari?"

"Just shut up and do it."

"What about our young friend here?" Faas motioned to a figure bound to a tree, his dark head sagging on his chest. Long, dark hair whipped around his battered face. Mateo!

My heart leapt for joy. He was alive!

Ari chuckled. "He's only bait for our real prize. Screw him."

I narrowed my eyes and pure hate welled up inside me. We'll see about that, asshole.

Struggling against the wind blowing hard in my face, I trudged through the trees, my boots sinking deeper and deeper into the snow. It was as if I was wading through quicksand, but determination pushed me forward. Mateo was less than five feet away. I could almost reach out and touch him. I could save him. I knew I could. Knew I would.

But then the cold air changed around me. It had been fresh and clean, but now it smelled foul and evil.

Something was here.

A dark cloaked figure and a wolf emerged together from behind the boulder. "At last, she's here."

Fear crushed my heart and squeezed the air out of my lungs. Shit, Velkan.

He pointed. "Right there, fools."

Ari scrambled to his feet and Faas whirled around, pulling his arm back, ready to launch a fireball at me.

Velkan held up his palm. "Wait." He looked at his wolf, then at Mateo, then at his wolf again.

"Kill him."

I screamed, thrashing back and forth

Someone put their palm over my mouth. "Salem, shhh. Wake up. You're having a nightmare."

My eyes flew open, and I stared into Gunnar's concerned eyes.

My wolves stood over me and Nico growled at Gunnar as if to say get your hands off her.

Gunnar slowly raised his hands. "Easy. I'm not hurting her, boy."

Gasping for breath, I looked up at my protective wolf. His upper lip was pulled back, and he took a menacing step toward Gunnar. "Nico, no. I'm…I'm all right."

Nico glanced down at me and narrowed his eyes as if he didn't believe me.

Gunnar scooted away from me as I sat up. I ran my fingers through my hair.

Tears blurred my vision, and I wrapped my arms around Nico's thick neck, burying my soft sobs.

"What's going on?" Ashton asked behind me.

I slowly released Nico and petted him. I glanced between him and Gunnar and counted to five before I spoke, trying to gather my wits about me. "I dreamt…of Mateo."

"Go on," Ashton said as he rubbed my back.

Gunnar gave me a sympathetic look. "What were Faas and Ari doing to him?"

"He was…tied…to a tree. He'd been beaten." I smiled through my silly tears. "But he was alive."

Ashton gave me a small hug. "So, why were you screaming if he was alive?"

I bit my lip and looked down at my trembling hands. Tears splashed on them. I didn't answer him for several deep breaths.

He nudged me. "Salem?"

"What's going on?" Rubbing her eyes, Ebony scooted next to Gunnar.

"She had a nightmare about Mateo," he said.

Ebony dropped her hands. "What happened, Salem? Please, tell us.

I glanced up at the ceiling. "Velkan. He came. He…he… ordered the demon wolf to kill him." I looked at her with my heart breaking. "Mateo…he couldn't…he couldn't defend himself. The wolf was about to rip him to pieces. That's when I woke up."

Ashton hugged me tightly, giving me strength, whispering in my ear, "Listen to me. It was a dream. That's all. Mateo's alive. You must have faith."

I nodded and disentangled myself from his embrace. "I want to believe you, but Velkan has shown me dreams before—"

Gunnar frowned. "Are you sure it was Velkan?" His tone sent a bucket of fear splashing all over me.

"Yes. Why do you think it was Ari or Faas who sent the dream?"

He shook his head. "No, but Balthazar might have."

I didn't want to go down that dark path. "But he wasn't in the dream."

"Does he need to be in it to send it?" he asked gently.

I scrubbed my face with hands. "I guess not, no. This sucks."

"War always does," he said grimly.

I dragged my fingers through my hair, trying to get the tangles out. "What do we do now?"

He shrugged. "What else? We eat the last remaining food—"

Ashton blurted. "Sorry, it's gone."

Gloria yawned. "Really? There's no food left at all?"

"No," Ashton said. "We'll have to hunt for it." He gave her a hard grin. "I doubt that your father will order a banquet for us."

"Only if we're the main dish," she quipped.

I sighed heavily. "I guess it's time for us to put our plan into place. Everyone ready?"

Ebony clasped Gunnar's hand. "Ready. Hades and I will fly over the mountain and then come around Faas' and Ari's flank."

Gunnar kissed her knuckles. "Come back to me."

"I will."

Gunnar stood, pulling her with him, and slapped his gut unhappily. "Well, I guess we go into battle with empty bellies." He released Ebony's hand and then stretched out his arms wide. "Hades, come forth."

Hades moved around on Gunnar's chest and then leaped from his body, turning into the little Catalan dragon I had grown to love and dropping to the ground after a graceful twist in the air.

He had landed right in front of me, and I put my arms around his thick neck. "You ready for this, buddy?"

He nuzzled my neck with his nose.

"I guess you are." I cupped his furry cheeks. "You watch out for Ebony, okay?"

Hades licked my face. I hugged him hard, hoping for all the world I wasn't sending him to his death.

I dragged myself to wearily to my feet.

Ebony hugged Gunnar. "Be careful. I can't lose you again."

He kissed her cheek. "You won't. You'd better come back to me, my queen."

Tears glistened in her eyes. "I will. I promise."

Ashton gave her a big hug, too. "To open the door, say Defenum."

She stared into his eyes. "See you soon."

He nodded. Ashton, Ebony, Gunnar, and Hades shared a history. They'd all fought together in the Great Supernatural War against Cormac and Ryker. It had been fierce and bloody.

By the look in their eyes, they were afraid history was going to repeat itself today.

Ebony tilted her head and stretched out her arm. "Come on, Hades. It's time to go."

The Catalan dragon hurried to her side. Ebony shifted into her bat, and Hades unfurled his wings. They flew away toward the entrance to the tunnel and the rest of us stood together, watching them until the shadows covered them.

I looked around the rest of the group and then down at my wolves. "I guess it's my turn." As I inhaled a deep breath, I touched all three of my wolves. "*Petriendo.*"

The tingling sensations rolled through me, and my spine arched as the power moved through me.

Gunnar tilted his head curiously. "So that spell really makes them disappear?"

I nodded. "For everyone else, yes, but I can still see them faintly. I have taken in some of their power."

Gunnar shook his head in smiling disbelief. "No wonder Calvin fears you so much."

"How long do you think it will take Hades and Ebony to fly over the mountain in this storm?" Gloria asked.

"Not long," Gunnar said. "We will to take the lanterns with us." He glanced between Ashton and Gloria. "But when Salem and I open the door, you must douse the light immediately."

"We will." Ashton grabbed a lantern off the wall.

Gloria carefully unhooked another one. "I hope this works."

"It's all we've got," I said solemnly.

Ashton and Gloria held up the lanterns, casting our shadows long against the wall.

"I'll go first." Ashton moved ahead of me and the wolves.

For once, I didn't argue with him. He carefully made his way down the tunnel, holding the lantern up high.

The demon wolves and I followed him. Interestingly enough, when under this spell, the wolves didn't cast shadows on the wall. They were like powerful wraiths. I could feel their power surging through me, turning my adrenaline up to eleven.

I glanced over my shoulder. Gloria was right behind me and was no longer carrying the lantern. Gunnar had it. She was breathing hard, and her eyes were wide. She was absolutely terrified, but still she went on. The only difference between us was she showed her fear while I buried mine. But if she put her ear to my chest, she'd hear my heart pounding louder than a thunderstorm. The only things keeping me calm were the power pushing through me and my sheer determination.

Mateo was out there, and I wasn't going to let him freeze to death or let the other wolf rip him to shreds.

Our footsteps echoed softly on the ground. My wolves didn't seem to be the least bit frightened. Nico was in front of the other two, slightly bigger than Remus and Luna. Their nails clicked on the floor, softer than our footsteps.

We seemed to go on forever and ever. Surely, Ebony and Hades had reached the end of the tunnel and were outside already. Once again, the tunnel walls became so narrow in places that we had to turn sideways to continue. Last time we had slept for a couple of hours, but if we stopped to rest this time, it would be a perfect chance for Faas and Ari to sneak up on us.

Gloria stumbled into me a couple of times. “Sorry. I’m just so tired.”

“It’s okay,” I mumbled. She wasn’t the only one. All I wanted to do was rest, but there wasn’t time to stop. My stomach grumbled for the millionth time, but I ignored it. More than once, I thought I heard the others’ tummies rumbling as loud as mine.

Ashton glanced over his shoulder. “We’re almost at the end. Be on guard. Ari has the ability to turn invisible.”

Now he tells me? I wiped my slick palms on my thighs.

Be calm Be calm Be calm

We finally reached the door. Outside, the enemy waited for us.

Time to find out whether my plan would work, or send us all to our death.

21

We all faced the cave door that would lead us out into the woods from where we could go on to Iredale Palace. Hopefully, Ebony and Hades were out there and still in one piece. My heart thundered, sending adrenaline through me like a raging inferno. I could feel the demon wolves' power simmering beneath the surface within me. I took a strong stance and lifted my chin high.

Gunnar handed his lantern to Gloria. "Remember, you need to douse it before I open this door."

She nodded. "I will." She opened the lantern's glass door and held it up to her face, ready to blow out the candle inside.

Ashton did the same with his.

Gunnar stepped to the door and looked over at me. "Ready?"

I braced my shoulders and placed my hands on Remus and Luna. Nico stood in front of us, as always. "Ready."

He motioned with his hand. "Come and stand next to me. We need them to see you."

"Stay here," I told my beloved wolves.

I left them and stood next to Gunnar, who squeezed my hand gently.

"We can do this."

I nodded, not sure whether I believed him, but I knew in my heart I would die trying. My mate, my friends, and countless other lives depended on me.

"*Defenum*," Gunnar whispered.

The lanterns immediately were doused. Darkness engulfed us like a shroud.

A crack splintered down the wall. Immediately cold air rushed in, whipping around us like angry sprites.

The door creaked as it slid open. Heavy flakes burst into the cave, as if trying to escape the cold.

I shielded my eyes with my palm against the stormy white stuff flurrying around me.

"Come on," Gunnar yelled over the wind.

He clutched my hand and dragged me out of the cave.

At first, I couldn't see anything.

Gunnar pointed. "Look."

I followed his finger, and my heart froze.

The same ball of fire I had seen in my dream blazed in the distance. Instinctively, I knew Mateo was there too, beaten and tortured. He needed me.

I clasped his arm. "Gunnar. It's them. Mateo's with them, I'm sure of it. I can't stay here. They're too far away. I don't think Ari and Faas can see us because of the storm." My voice came out in loud, rapid fire.

"Damn it," he grumbled.

Ashton, Gloria, and my wolves came up alongside us.

"Okay, new plan," Ashton said as he unsheathed his sword. "We go to them."

The wind blew around us as if it had an evil purpose.

I stuck out my hand. "Together."

One by one, the other laid their palms on top of mine. "We do this as a team."

"Okay, maybe I've come late to the party," Gloria said. "But what exactly are we doing?"

Ashton sighed. "We're going to be joining Hades and Ebony and sneaking behind Ari and Faas."

She glanced up at the sky. "That's what I was afraid you were going to say."

"It's okay, Gloria," I reassured her. I'll draw them out and then you attack. Once they're busy fighting us, I'll unleash my demon wolves."

Gunnar looked at each of us. "Don't forget, I have another side, right?" He flashed out his black wings.

"You do?" Gloria asked quakingly.

He nodded. "I was my father's killer for a long time and I'm going to have to draw on that power to fight these guys. Just don't freak out when you see me change. I won't hurt any of you."

Fear flashed in Gloria's eyes. "You make it sound like you're scary-looking."

"Yep. I'm terrifying." He spread his wings and flew into the angry storm.

We all looked at each other. Ashton had an uneasy look on his face.

"You've seen him when he's like that, haven't you?" I asked.

He nodded. "He's worse than terrifying. Come on, Salem, you'd better get going."

I scanned the sky, looking for Gunnar or whatever monster he had become, but I didn't see him.

Ashton and Gloria disappeared into the storm.

My demon wolves looked up at me curiously.

"Okay, guys. Let's go." I headed toward the trees with my wolves fanning out behind me.

I gasped. As usual, they didn't cast shadows, but last time, they had left footprints in the snow. But now they weren't leaving any. What was that about? This was so weird, but it didn't matter. We had an advantage.

The hair on the back of my neck stood straight up and I had a feeling we were being watched. Not by Gunnar, or Ebony, or even Hades.

No, this was something different.

Something evil.

Velkan, Balthazar, perhaps even my uncle.

Goosebumps broke out all over me, and it wasn't from the cold.

Don't panic Don't panic Don't panic

I looked wildly around me, but the snow was blinding and I couldn't see a damn thing.

I did my best to shake the feeling. I slipped from tree to tree with my wolves following right behind me.

The fiery light was burning brighter and brighter. I could see a tall, blond mountain man through the trees. Faas. It had to be Faas.

My heartbeat thundered, and I shivered underneath my heavy coat.

Crap, this was just like my damn nightmare.

Oh, no.

Mateo.

I stumbled through the snow, falling again and again, but I didn't care. Calmness had completely left me.

Just like in my dream, it was as if I was sinking into quicksand.

"Nico," I gasped. I wasn't sure if he even would understand me, but I had to try.

Nico stared at me with his deep red eyes.

"There's a man—over there—tied up by that fire. PleasePlease-Please, protect him."

Nico turned and ran through the trees. Panting, I dragged myself to my feet and leaned my back against a tree.

"Get yourself together," I grumbled underneath my breath.

You have the power You have the power You have the power

I kept repeating the affirmation over and over in my head like a broken record.

I started off again, slipping in and out of the trees. My pace slowed, but I wasn't falling thigh deep into the snow anymore.

Luna and Remus stayed right with me.

I got closer and closer.

Just like in my dream, Ari was huddled on the ground with his arms wrapped around his neck and Faas was tossing his fireball into the air like a juggler.

Mateo was slumped over, tied to the same tree I had seen in my dream, but now he wasn't alone. Nico was with him. Mateo's thick, curly hair blew around him, and I could see his beard had iced over. Damn it, he was freezing to death.

Ari glared at Faas. "Will you hurry up and warm up the damn boulder?"

Faas laughed. "Freezing Ari?"

"Just shut up and do it."

"What about our young friend here?" Faas motioned toward Mateo.

Ari chuckled. "He's only bait for our real prize. Screw him."

Their words sent fear whizzing through me like a bomb.

The blood drained from my face, pumping into my heart harder, making it swell and swell until I thought it would burst. Shit, was I having a heart attack?

Then things got worse. Once again, the fresh, clean air turned foul.

Remus and Luna growled softly. They smelled the change, too.

Right on cue, Velkan came out from around the boulder with the other wolf.

"At last, she's here."

Beads of sweat broke out across my forehead.

Ari scrambled to his feet, and Faas whirled around, pulling his arm back, ready to shoot a fireball at me.

Velkan held up his palm. "Wait." He looked at his wolf, then pointed at Mateo. "Kill him."

This time I didn't wake up.

Nico stood in front of Mateo, snarling, his hair bristling.

The other wolf hesitated, unsure what to do.

I stepped out from behind the tree and I was out in the open. The wind whipped my hair around my face and I raised my palm.

"Don't do it," Velkan warned. "You say one word and Faas will fry your mate."

Two figures dropped out of the sky like rockets, smashing into Ari and Faas. Hades pinned Ari to the ground and bit his neck. Blood splashed onto Hades' blond fur.

"Get this damned creature off me. Get him *off*." Ari howled as he beat on Hades' side.

I would have almost felt sorry for Ari if he hadn't been pure evil.

Faas and Gunnar wrestled on the ground like a furious snowball.

"Kill her mate, you fool." Velkan yelled as he drew his sword.

Shit, if the wolf didn't kill Mateo, then Velkan would.

"Remus, Luna, attack."

Remus and Luna lunged at the demon.

Velkan whirled around, but he was too slow. Remus bit into his leg and the demon cried out.

He slashed his sword at Remus, but missed, and his blade went through the air.

Velkan motioned toward Mateo. "Damn you, wolf, can't you just kill him?"

The wolf moved around Nico, but Nico held his ground, growling.

With one final desperate scream I cried out, "*Morphello—*"

Shriek Shriek

Sharp pain slashed through my jacket, slicing into my flesh. I staggered and fell to the ground, face first. I turned my head. Crap, it was a harpy.

Luna charged and smashed into the harpy just as the thing was readying to slash me again. Luna knocked the harpy to the ground and ripped out her throat in one swift, violent bite.

The harpy gurgled and died.

Velkan broke free of Remus. His eyes widened. "The demon wolves."

Oh, God no. Don't enslave them.

I raised my hand. "*Morphello Refulsi.*" Pink tingles swept over my fingers and lifted the last wolf off the ground. I wouldn't let Velkan enslave my other wolves again. I fanned my hand around the battlefield and repeated the spell. All four wolves were encased in the pink tingles.

"You bitch. You'll pay for this." Velkan lifted his sword and threw it at Mateo, hitting him in the chest. Mateo cried out and slumped to the side.

I screamed. "Nooooo!"

Velkan laughed diabolically. Then he faded away, leaving a trail of blood.

All the power drained out of me. My arm shook, and I couldn't keep the wolves suspended. They fell into the snow one by one.

Sobbing, I crawled through the snow toward Mateo. A burning sensation seeped into my blood and pulsed through me. Pain gripped me, locking me in place, preventing me from moving.

I lifted my head. "Mateo." Something dripped down my chin and I realized I was choking on my own blood.

"Mateo..." I gurgled once more.

But he didn't look up. The sword was lodged deep in his chest. He was soaked in blood.

Ari cursed and screamed, trying to get Hades off him. Gunnar and Faas were squaring off. I blinked. Gunnar's eyes had turned a dark, evil red and his face looked more like a skull. He had long fingernails that looked like they were coated with blood. I almost didn't recognize him.

Faas was swaying on his feet, but another fireball formed in his hand.

"You can't kill me," Gunnar said. "I'll only heal myself."

That's right. Gunnar was the Dark Demon Healer. He could heal not only himself but others.

"Maybe so." Faas flashed out his wings. "But I can still kill your friends."

He flung a fireball at Mateo, who immediately burst into flames.

"You bastard." Gunnar raced over to Mateo.

I screamed again, spitting more blood. Nico, Remus, and Luna huddled around me, licking my face and the wounds on my back. The fourth wolf lay quietly in the snow, not moving.

Faas flew into the sky, abandoning Ari to his fate. I looked up to see a fireball streaming toward me.

"Move," I whispered to my demon wolves.

They tugged on my coat and jeans, trying to get me out of the line of fire, but they were too late. Heat slammed into me and I cried out. The last thing I thought before I lost consciousness was that at least Mateo and I would be together.

22

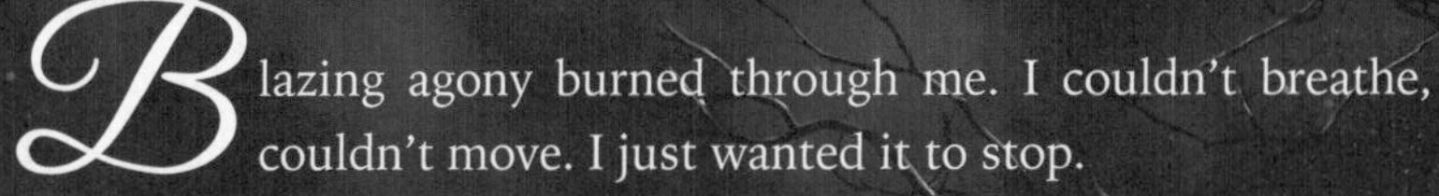

Blazing agony burned through me. I couldn't breathe, couldn't move. I just wanted it to stop.

Fog swirled around in my brain and I felt like I was floating higher and higher, almost as if I was walking on air.

Something touched me. It felt cool and soft. The burning pain abated, as if it was slowly being drawn out of me.

"Salem, can you hear me?"

A distant male voice called to me. It was a musical whistle. Was this Heaven? Was the voice of the Archangel Michael or Raphael? Had I died?

I tossed my head back and forth.

"Salem, come back to me." The male voice was getting closer, and suddenly I recognized it.

It wasn't an archangel.

My eyes fluttered open, and I found myself staring up at Gunnar. His tired eyes were filled with worry and he looked nothing like he had when he was fighting Faas. He had a dark shadow of a stubble beard, and his white hair was tousled as if he been running his fingers through it constantly. But damn, he was a sight for sore eyes.

"Gunnar?" My voice was raspy.

He smiled wearily and sighed. "Welcome back to the land of the living."

I looked around and realized I wasn't outside. I was back in the cave.

Tears slid down my cheeks. "And Mateo?"

"Look for yourself."

I followed his gaze and saw Mateo sleeping peacefully next to me. The terrible bruises on his handsome face had disappeared. His chest moved up and down. I could hear the sweet sound of his breath.

"Am I dreaming?" I whispered, slowly stretching out my hand. It looked badly sunburned.

"No. He's alive, but it was touch and go for a while."

"It was?" Confusion swam in my brain. "I thought…I thought he was dead." Grief swelled up in my throat like a bullfrog. "I thought Faas…"

I closed my eyes, not wanting to picture that image in my head again.

"He did," Gunnar admitted.

"Then I don't understand," I whispered. Not that I wasn't grateful. Mateo was breathing and alive and perfect.

"He's a healer." Ebony sat down next to him, along with Hades. "So is this little guy. Hades eats dark magic. He's the one that healed Mateo, actually."

Ebony rubbed Gunnar's back. "But Gunnar healed you."

"It was tough. Between Faas' fireball and the harpy's poison, I wasn't sure you would make it. You still need to rest some." He studied me. "I can't take all the credit for healing you, you know."

"You lost me again," I sighed.

"Salem, there was something within you that was healing you from the inside. I only drew it out more. I believe it had something to do with all four demon wolves."

Something soft nuzzled my cheek. I stared up into Luna's soft red eyes. "Hey, girl." I gave her a grateful smile. "Did you help heal me?"

The other three wolves and Hades all surrounded me.

"They haven't left your side." Ebony gestured toward a wolf that seemed more timid than the other three. "Gloria says the fourth wolf is named Bella."

"Hello, Bella."

Bella licked my cheek, and I laughed.

I forced myself to sit up slowly and winced. My skin felt tight, as if I had a terrible sunburn. I crossed my legs gingerly and rolled up my sleeve on one arm. It was dark pink. I cocked my eyebrow. "I take it my whole body looks like I've turned into Petunia Pig?"

Gunnar nodded. "You're lucky to be alive, Salem. You're still healing. From what I've observed, though, in a day or so, you should be fine again."

I gently picked up Mateo's limp hand. He let out a loud snore. "May I wake him?"

Gunnar shook his head. "Not yet, please. The longer he sleeps, the better and more quickly his body will heal."

I rubbed my forehead. "How long have I been out, anyway?"

"A couple of days." Ebony clasped my hand. Tears glistened in her eyes. "There were times we thought we'd lost you, but there's a determination in you that wouldn't be denied."

"I agree," Gunnar said. "The wolves continued to lick your hands and your face. There's something about their saliva that contains some kind of healing power, I think." He chuckled as he petted Remus' head. "They weren't giving up on you either."

Ebony squeezed my hand. "Your demon wolves are amazing, Salem. I had no idea they possessed such power."

I leaned my head against Nico. "Neither did I." I frowned. "Do you think Velkan or Calvin know about it?"

Gunnar shrugged. "I have no idea, but honestly, I suspect those two were only interested in the wolves' killing power."

"Figures," I muttered.

I scanned the cave. "Where are Gloria and Ashton?"

"Out hunting," Gunnar said. "They should be back soon."

Alarm bells rang inside my head. "Is it safe for them to be out there? What happened to Faas and Ari?"

"We don't know," Ebony said grimly. "Hades stopped tearing into Ari when Faas threw the fireball at Mateo. He disappeared, and we don't know if Hades killed him or not."

I rubbed my forehead. "Well, shoot. That's not good."

Gunnar stretched his arms and yawned. "I'd like to think the bastard's dead, but I wouldn't count on it. He's probably deep in a hole, nursing his wounds. We definitely haven't seen the last of him."

"You don't think Faas helped him escape?" I asked.

Gunnar exhaled a sharp burst of air. "No way. Those two only think of number one. My dad forced them to work as a team, but now that he's gone, they're back to caring only about themselves."

I stroked Mateo's soft hair, wishing he'd wake. He was so beautiful, and I wanted to stare into his dark eyes again. "Why hasn't Stefan come to drag Ari and Faas back to the Hollows?"

"I don't know," Gunnar got up and shook out his legs. "I think he's waiting for you to reclaim your crown before he sets things right."

My gut tightened. "But what if I can't?"

"You will." Ebony nudged me gently in the ribs. "You're a badass, Salem. You always have been, even back when you were growing up in foster care."

I elbowed her in return. "How would you know? You weren't there."

She tilted her head and laughed sweetly. "I didn't have to be."

The door slid open. I immediately tensed and covered Mateo's body with my own. I wasn't losing him again. Gunnar whirled around and Ebony jumped up next to him. The demon wolves all stepped in front of Mateo, poised for an attack, their hackles bristling, baring their teeth.

Cold air rushed into the room.

Gloria swooped inside as her wolf and shook her fur. The demon wolves relaxed and wagged their tails.

"Anyone hungry?" Ashton came in behind her, carrying thick slices of meat. "I just gutted a deer outside and we'll be able to fill our empty bellies."

"Don't you think that will draw attention to us?" Gunnar frowned and then hurried over to the door. "*Defenum.*" Once again, the cave door creaked and slid shut.

"I'm not worried," Ashton shrugged. "They already know we're here. At least this way we'll eat."

Ebony looked at Ashton. "Any signs of Faas or Ari?"

"Nothing. Gloria and I couldn't find any tracks." Ashton carefully dropped the strips of meat onto the floor and I noticed that there was a small crudely built firepit that hadn't been there before. "The Winter Solstice is less than two days, Salem." He looked at me levelly. "I think Calvin's waiting for you to come to him."

I squeezed Mateo's warm hand, wishing for all the world he would sit up and kiss me. Right now, I needed his strength. I sighed heavily. "If I don't show up, he'll kill my aunt Remi and Quint, won't he?"

"You know it," he said softly.

The demon wolves hovered around the strips of meat, licking their chops hungrily.

I gestured toward the pit. "Aren't you going to smoke us out in here?" I didn't want Mateo choking on the fumes.

"I'll keep the door ajar. We have to eat if we want to win this war, especially you, Salem."

Nico sniffed and tugged on the piece of meat.

Ashton frowned and yanked it out of his mouth. "Hey now, wait your turn."

Nico growled, and his ears flattened.

I snapped my fingers warningly. "Nico."

Nico looked at me and stopped growling, but I had a feeling if I hadn't been here, he would have attacked.

"On second thought, I think you guys have earned this." Ashton quickly tossed them each several long strips of raw meat and my wolves dove in greedily.

He got up. "I'll be right back with some more meat and start cooking it."

Ebony strolled over to the fire pit that had some stones and bits of wood. "Hades, will you please come and light the fire?"

The little Catalan Dragon trotted over to the fire pit and exhaled, sending a gust of fire over the stones and sticks. A blaze ignited, giving off warmth.

"Thanks, buddy," Ebony said.

Ashton returned with more deer meat. "As soon as Mateo's up and about, I think we should start off. Things are moving apace. I didn't realize it, but the cemetery and the mausoleum's not too far from here."

My eyes widened. "Really? I thought it would be inside the Moon Kingdom."

"Apparently, the kings were buried away from the common folk in their own special place. Gloria and I stumbled upon it when we were hunting this deer. It's called Moonlight Gardens." He cleared his throat. "Your parents are both buried there." His words struck me hard.

The thought of seeing my parents' grave unnerved me. Something happened that I didn't think would happen. The sudden urge to cry swelled inside me. Eyes burning, throat swelling, and heart squeezing. I blinked the stupid tears and took a deep breath, struggling to stay in control, trying not to think of all the times I was shuffled from foster home to foster home. All because my selfish, evil uncle robbed me of life with loving parents and landed me in a childhood of loneliness and despair.

"I'm sorry," he said as he cut up the meat. "I didn't mean to upset you."

I wiped my cheeks, feeling like an idiot. "No, it's okay. It's just...hard. It seems like Calvin has taken so much from me."

Gloria sat next to me. She had shifted from her wolf and had put on her pink sweater and black yoga pants. She'd even put on pink lipstick. As always, she looked beautiful.

"That's because he has. My father took everything from me, too," she said. She looked down at her hands. "Did you know he murdered my mother?"

My eyes widened. "Wha-at?"

She nodded unhappily. "He always denied it, but Hayley told me the truth. He gave my mom the same poison he gave your parents."

I frowned. "Why?"

"Because he's a fucking asshole," a deep male voice whispered. The air whisked out of my lungs to hear that husky male voice that I had never hoped to hear again.

Mateo slowly sat up and we stared at each other as if we couldn't believe the other was alive.

My heart thundered, sending blood racing through me. His gaze turned my entire body hot, and I ached for him to touch me. But what if he wasn't completely healed? Gunnar said he needed more time to rest.

I scanned Mateo's handsome face, mesmerized by everything about him—the dark slash of his eyebrows, his deep brown eyes, the straight line of his nose, and his beard that outlined the rugged squareness of his jaw. He was everything to me. I wanted to pinch myself to make sure I was awake and not dreaming. Part of me thought that any second Velkan or Balthazar would jump out and say April Fools.

"Mateo." I could barely get the word out with my tongue tumbling over his name.

He flashed me his wonderful, heart-melting smile. "Salem."

I wanted to tell him I loved him, but once again, those three little words lodged in my throat like a stuck crust of dry bread.

What was wrong with me? Anton said that would be the hardest thing for to me to do, and go figure, so far it was proving harder than fighting harpies and demons.

He slipped his calloused hand around my neck and pulled me close. "God, you're a sight for sore eyes. I've missed you. Dreaming of kissing you again was what got me through those dark times."

"Then kiss me."

23

Time stopped for me. I barely noticed the cave or the venison crackling on the small stove. Smoke drifted around the room, making Mateo look mysterious.

Someone—maybe Gunnar—said *Defenum*. the door opened a little and smoke seeped out of the cave.

Gloria wisely got up and left us alone. Gunnar frowned and opened his mouth as if to reprimand me and Mateo for engaging in too much physical activity after we'd just been healed. But Ebony cleared her throat and shook her head.

Mateo didn't seem to notice anyone but me. Without hesitation, he pulled me into his lap and I could feel his groin pulsing against me. My heart was thumping like a wild thing. I stared into his eyes, not sure what he would do next.

His lips brushed over mine and then he pushed my mouth open with his tongue. I sighed. It was heavenly. I had missed this so much. His kiss was tender but then turned domineering, desperate, determined.

I slipped my hands around his neck and the next thing I knew he stood, wobbling, lifting me into his arms.

"Mateo," I gasped. "What are you doing?" I couldn't keep the giggle of surprise and eager anticipation out of my voice. Damn, I wanted this. Wanted him.

"Doing what I've dreamed about for months," he growled.

"I don't think that's wise," Gunnar interrupted. "You've only just been healed and you can barely walk."

"What I'm going to do doesn't require walking." Mateo carried me away from the soft lantern light.

Gunnar headed over to us. "I must insist—"

He paused. All four demon wolves stood in his way like a blockade.

"You're going to be sorry," Gunnar promised.

"He's going to be sorry if he tries to get in my way," Mateo muttered in my ear.

I cupped his rugged cheek. "Are you sure you're up to this? Maybe he's right."

"Are you questioning my manhood?" he asked gruffly.

"No, never."

"Good, because I'm going to burst if I don't take you now, my queen."

"I'm not the queen yet."

"You've always been my queen." Mateo slowly lowered himself to the ground, still cradling me close to his chest. We were quite a distance from the others, enough that they couldn't hear what we were about to do. Or at least I hoped they wouldn't.

When he kissed me again, tremors spread through my arms, down to the very tips of my fingers that were curling in his shirt. I spread my lips wider beneath his, allowing him into the warmth and wetness. Suddenly, I didn't care if the rest of my team could see or hear us. All I cared about was tasting him again, having him hold me in his arms again. He traced delicate patterns with his tongue in and around my mouth, and I shivered wantonly beneath his seductive magic.

"I want to feel your skin on mine." He planted kissed down my chin to my ear.

The next thing I knew, he was unzipping my coat.

"Eager, are you?" I asked, as he helped me shed my coat.

"You have no idea." He tugged my shirt over my head and before I could say another word, his mouth was on my nipple, sucking it through my bra.

I gasped and raked my fingers through his thick hair. I arched my back shamelessly, allowing me to take more of my flesh into his hot, greedy mouth. Whoosh. I was on my back and Mateo was moving his hands over my skin, unclasping my bra and unzipping my jeans. He broke his mouth away from my soaked bra and tugged at my jeans. I quickly tossed my bra aside, feeling reckless and abandoned.

He slid my jeans down to my ankles, then cursed as he pushed off my boots. Finally I lay naked, staring up at him, watching as shed his sweater, jeans, and boots. I could see every inch of him, even in the darkness. It had to be the power of my demon wolves. I smiled wickedly as I eagerly waited for his mouth and hands to be roaming all over me.

Mateo didn't disappoint. He kissed me hard as his hands explored my feverish body. Blood pumped down to my inner thighs. I moaned when he slipped his fingers into my secret curls, stroking me until I was shivering and panting loudly. Then he stopped kissing my lips, moving the sweet torture down past the hollow of my breasts to my belly, turning my body into pure liquid fire, flowing and silky and smooth. His mouth pressed against my soft mound and I whimpered.

Heat and pleasure rolled over me in long undulating waves, bold and intense, and I dug my nails into the cold dirt. The sensations grew more and more intense, and I opened my thighs wider and arched my hips as he dipped his tongue deeper and deeper. The first tinge of my orgasm rushed over me, and I cried out his name.

"I've only just begun, my sweet mate." He placed his hands firmly on my hips while his lips and tongue took me places I only dreamed of.

I shuddered repeatedly as I exploded with pleasure, but that wasn't all that was happening. Something was building inside me —a power that got stronger and stronger each time Mateo kissed me. I thrashed my head back and forth, not understanding what was happening, but my skin no longer felt cracked and burnt, but silky and hot.

"You're so passionate," he whispered. "Am I hurting you?"

"Seriously? No."

He climbed up on my body and with firm hands moved my thighs apart, settling his hips between mine.

I ran the tips of my fingers up and down his back. "I've missed you so much. This is the moment of I've dreamed of."

"Making love in a cave?"

"I like to keep things interesting," I laughed, then squeezed his buttocks hard.

He gasped. "You little minx. You always keep me guessing." He kissed me long and hard, making me forget everything except him.

"I love you," he whispered, as he planted kisses down my throat.

I almost was about to finally say those same little words when he pressed his hips forward and slid his cock deep into my channel. I sucked in my breath, waiting for my body to accommodate his large size, unable to move. It had been so long since I'd been with him that I had forgotten how well-endowed he was and how much he turned me into a blubbering mess.

"You're tensing." He pushed my hair back. "Move with me, Salem. Relax."

He glided his flesh back and forth, withdrawing and thrusting, withdrawing and thrusting, with long, silky strokes. I dug my fingers into his shoulders, hanging on for the desperate ride. The pain turned into pleasure and something inside of me clicked over.

"Harder," I pleaded.

"As you wish."

He kissed me as he increased his pace, slamming his hips into mine, plunging his cock deeper and deeper. His long, dark hair teased my sensitive skin. Flesh ground against flesh. Heat slipped into heat. The pace was breathtaking. I dug my heels into the hard ground and met him thrust for thrust. White spots danced in front of my eyes.

Once again, he stoked the flames of pleasure within me, making the fire burn higher and higher. My body tightened around his, one spasm after another, diving into a pool of heaven. I locked my ankles around his thrusting hips. Bright torrents of ecstasy strummed through me, sweeping me into another hot steamy orgasm that left me spent, drained, and smiling.

And that wasn't all. The power he had kindled grew stronger.

I cupped his ass, making him gasp again. I was vaguely aware that he had tilted his head back and, with one final thrust, spilled his hot seed inside me. His arms trembled and then he collapsed on top of me, still pulsing in me.

"Mateo." I clasped his hot cheeks. "Are you okay?"

He exhaled a gasp of breath. "Are you serious?"

"Yes." I unlocked my ankles, afraid I had hurt him, wishing I had insisted that we wait.

"Salem." He panted and then kissed the crook of my neck. "Every time we do this, you take a little bit more of my soul. I honestly don't think I will ever get enough of you. You've stolen my heart."

"Me too," I said softly, wishing I had the courage to tell him how I felt.

He sighed and I could almost hear the disappointment buried in his exhale.

"Mateo." I moved my fingertips up and down his sweaty back. "Did you hear what Ashton said?"

He didn't answer for several long heartbeats, and I didn't know if he had heard me. Maybe he had fallen asleep. "Mateo?"

"Yeah, I heard him. You mean about the cemetery, right?"

I stroked his hair. "How long had you been awake?"

"Long enough. I just couldn't open my eyes. But I wasn't going to sleep, knowing you were so near."

"Let me guess." I looked down at him fondly. "You smelled my scent."

He kissed the top of my shoulder. "I could find you anywhere."

"So...back to the cemetery. Have you ever been there?"

He got up on his forearms. "Unfortunately, too many times. You'd be walking into a trap."

Frustration fluttered inside me. "Calvin has been throwing surprise parties for us the whole way. Why should the cemetery be any different?"

He stared at me sadly. "Because you have to go into the first king's mausoleum by yourself. Remember?" His voice held a hint of fear.

I tilted my chin up high. "But I won't be alone."

Uneasiness flared in his deep brown eyes. "What do you mean? If you don't come into the mausoleum on your own, he'll kill both Remi and Quint. Is that what you want?"

I shook my head. "No, of course not. But my demon wolves will be with me."

He glared at me. "Salem, you're not listening."

"No, you don't understand. Let me tell you about my wolves." I quickly told him all about them, including the way I could make them invisible.

"Damn. No wonder Calvin wants you out of the picture. He hasn't been able to do shit with the wolves, and he's been trying for years."

"So I've heard." I bit my lip. I wasn't sure I should tell him about my power getting stronger with his lovemaking, but he was my mate. "And there's something else, too."

"What? You're okay, aren't you?" Fear echoed in his words.

"Yes, I'm fine. In fact, I'm better than fine. Our mating has awakened fresh power in me. I feel stronger. My body feels like it's healed."

He laughed. "Yeah, I have that effect on women."

"Mateo! I'm serious." I pinched his tight ass.

"Ow. Hey, I'm sorry. But now that you mention it, there's something I need to tell you. I thought I was imagining it, but…I thought I could feel my body healing."

"Is that normal?"

"No, it's not, but when have we ever done anything normal?"

I took a deep breath. "I think I'm ready to go to the cemetery now." My gut roared in protest, making my cheeks burn.

Mateo chuckled. "Not until we get some food in our bellies. I'm starving." He slowly pulled out of me and rolled to the side.

I laughed, but it was small and nervous. For once, eating didn't seem important.

He picked up my hand and kissed my wrist. "I won't let anything happen to you in the cemetery. I'd protect you with my life."

"And I would you." Those three little words were hovering on the tip of my tongue.

Why couldn't I just say them, tell him how I really felt about him?

God, was I really that much of a pansy ass?

24

The smell of cooking meat swirled down the tunnel toward us. My stomach growled again.

Mateo laughed. "Really hungry, are you, Mate?"

I cupped his face. "Always…for you."

His eyes turned passionate and he kissed me. I clung to him, never wanting to let go. I wished I could persuade him to return to the safety of somewhere like Legacy, but I knew he was a fierce warrior and would never agree.

He broke off the kiss when my stomach made yet another annoying grumble and pressed his forehead against mine. "I guess I should get you something to eat."

I inhaled his warm, spicy breath and exhaled contently. "I wish I could stay here entangled with you."

He kissed the top of my forehead. "We'll do that again soon enough, I promise."

We slowly unwound from each other, and my heavy heart sank in my chest. Silently, we put on our clothes, but I couldn't keep my fears to myself.

I pressed my palms on his chest, feeling his beating heart. "May I please ask you to do something for me?"

"Anything," he whispered, as he wrapped his muscular arms around me.

"Will you return to Legacy Academy and stay with Anton?"

"What?"

I laid my head on his chest. "I couldn't bear to have you taken from me again." My voice cracked as the fear loomed over me.

He lifted my chin and looked deep into my eyes. "You know I can't do that."

I put my hands on his cheeks. "Promise me you won't do anything that will get you killed, at least."

He brushed his lips over mine. "Salem, I will do anything to protect you, even risk my life."

I hugged him desperately. "I can't lose you."

He stroked my hair. "You won't."

I lifted my head and stared up at him. "How can you be so sure?"

"Because I have faith in you." He kissed me softly. "You have the power to save us all."

I bit my lip, not sure I quite believed him.

He put his arm around my shoulder. "Come on, let's go see what Ashton's cooking up for us."

We emerged from the tunnel. My wolves were stretched out near the fire. Nico raised his head as we headed over to the fire pit.

Ebony gave me a knowing smile, and immediately two burning rosettes heated my cheeks. I avoided looking at the others.

Gunnar looked between us. "Your color has returned to normal. I take it back. I believe your mating was the last step in healing you both."

He returned to discussing something with Ebony that I couldn't hear. Neither he nor any of the others seemed the least bit taken back about what Mateo and I had been doing, but the blush still blooming on my cheeks ran all the way down to my squirming toes.

Mateo kissed my hot cheek. "Mating is definitely good for the soul."

Ashton looked up and gave us a teasing smile. "I bet you two are hungry."

Gloria frowned and elbowed him in the ribs. "Ashton!"

He shrugged. "Sorry."

"Yeah, we're starved," Mateo said as he sat down, pulling me with him.

Ashton handed each of us strips of venison. I bit into the meat and it practically melted in my mouth.

"Mmm. Ashton, this is delicious." I licked my fingers appreciatively.

He grinned. "Glad you like it."

"I didn't know you could cook. I always thought your servants did it for you."

He winked. "Most of the time they do, but I love to barbecue and cook wild game. You should see what I can do when I have some proper seasonings."

I stuffed myself with meat, not sure when I would get my next meal or if there even would be another one.

Ashton stood. "Are you two done eating?"

Mateo slapped his gut. "It was delicious. I can't eat another bite."

"Me either," I agreed.

Ashton headed toward the door. "I'm going to get some snow and put out the fire. I've wrapped up some barbecued meat and put it in cook's backpack for later, in case we get hungry."

I guess this meant we were leaving, and it was showtime, whether I was ready or not.

I looked at my beautiful wolves. "Last journey, guys. Are you ready?"

They stood around me, wagging their tails.

I smiled, praying they would all survive. "Okay. *Petriendo.*"

The wolves faded away. I stretched out my arms as their power flowed into me.

Mateo looked around the cave wildly. "Where did they go?"

I dropped my arms. "They're standing right in front of you. You can't see them?"

He shook his head. "No."

"Weird. I thought as my mate, maybe you would."

"I think it's because he's not Unseelie," Gunnar said.

"What do you mean?" Mateo looked at me questioningly.

I forgot that he didn't know. "Oh. Yeah...well...the reason the wolves and I are bonded is because I have Unseelie blood."

"What?!" He stepped back with a look of horror on his face.

My heart sank, and I looked down at my boots. I hadn't expected him to have this type of reaction.

Gunnar looked at him curiously. "You didn't know the first king's mother was an Unseelie?"

Mateo shook his head. "No. I didn't. Why can't Calvin control the wolves, then?"

"I'm not sure exactly." I cleared my throat and looked at him uncomfortably. "For some reason, the power within the Unseelie blood skipped Calvin and came to me."

He studied me and I held my breath, terrified he would not accept me. I turned away, not wanting to see the disgust in his eyes instead of love.

He clasped my chin and gently turned it, forcing me to look at him. "I don't know what I'm supposed to do here. I have fought the Unseelie and now I find you possess this same blood."

My lower lip trembled, waiting for him to reject me.

Hard, frantic breaths escaped my stiff lips as I waited for him to respond. Finally, he slipped his hand through my hair and pulled me to him. "But you know what? It doesn't really matter. You're mine, and I lost my heart to you the minute I saw you."

I smiled through my tears, wrapped my arms around his neck, and kissed him hard and deep until someone cleared their throat.

Within half an hour, we had left the tunnel and were heading out into the forest again. Overhead, the clouds were dreary, hiding the sun. The air was crisp and cold, but luckily, it hadn't started snowing again.

Ashton pointed. "About a mile past those trees is the cemetery."

I clutched my backpack, not wanting to think about who we might meet along the way.

Mateo scanned the sky and the forest. "Keep your eyes peeled for an ambush."

My demon wolves fanned in front of Mateo and I, invisible to everyone except me.

Hades trotted between Gunnar and Ebony, while Ashton and Gloria guarded the rear.

The trek through the forest was a short one. When we came out of the trees, I laid my eyes on the cemetery that was behind Iredale Palace. I had only seen the Palace from the front; from the back it was dismal, especially under the bleak skies. The gray stone curtain wall and towers cast a shadow over the cemetery. Guards walked along the curtain wall with swords drawn and bows and arrows strapped to their back. I didn't see how we could possibly sneak inside.

Some kind of commotion suddenly broke out on the walls, and the guards ran toward the front. Cries could be heard overhead. I wasn't sure what was going on, but it gave us an advantage.

"Move, *move*." Mateo motioned with his arm. "This is our chance."

We sprinted across the field as fast as we could. More cries erupted from Iredale Palace. It almost sounded like a battle. Ashton's dad? Was King Christopher leading the Tundra Kingdom in an attack against Iredale Palace?

A ten-foot-tall spiked metal gate surrounded the cemetery. Rather than tombstones, the cemetery had stone mausoleums with golden gates. The largest one was in the middle. Was that for the first king?

We ran along the fence until we came to the main gate, trying to keep away from prying eyes.

I sucked in deep breaths. "This is where I go in. The Rose Box is in the first king's mausoleum."

"You're not going in there alone." Mateo opened the creaking gate. "I'm coming with you."

I placed my hand on his chest. "No, you have to stay here. Balthazar's waiting inside for me. He'll kill you if he sees you. I must go alone."

He gritted his teeth. "Damn it, Salem. I'm not prepared to lose you again."

"Please, Mateo, you have to guard the outside. Besides, I won't be going alone. My wolves will be with me."

Cries and yells rang out around the building. Guards with swords high over their heads and wolves rushed toward us.

Mateo drew his sword and exhaled. "All right." He gestured with his weapon. "Go. Now."

I didn't hesitate. With arms and legs pumping, I raced as fast as I could toward the largest mausoleum. But a small mausoleum caught my eye. It didn't have a golden door. Just a plain wooden one. I read the names—King Andre Willis and his beloved wife, Queen Libby. My unshed tears made their escape and a ragged, angry sob escaped from pressed lips. I took a step toward the mausoleum, wanting to spend time with them. This was closest I had ever gotten to them.

"Salem, go," a male voice urged. I looked up and saw Mateo's determined face, gesturing with his arm. I wished he were here with me.

My wolves followed me. I didn't know if the mausoleum would even be open, but I had to try.

I ran up the steps two at a time.

Clank Clank Clank

I glanced over my shoulder. Gunnar, Ashton and Mateo were already battling the guards, white sparks from their swords flying into the air. I wanted to help them, but I had a job to do. This was the moment I had been waiting for. I pulled on the golden doors that were etched with wolves and angels. They yielded.

This was all way, way too easy.

Definitely a trap.

Nico snarled and stepped in front of me.

"It's okay, boy."

Nico led the wolves slowly into the enormous vault that was bigger than my old trailer. I stepped inside.

Bam

The doors slammed behind me.

"Finally. I was wondering when you were going to get here."

I gasped, and my heart skidded to a halt.

Balthazar stood in the corner of the mausoleum. His black hair flared over his shoulders and again he was shirtless, wearing only black leather pants and high boots. I swear he thought he was a rock star.

He looked at my wolves. "I see you have returned my valuable prizes to me." His evil, smooth voice sent a chill down my arms, down my spine, down my legs, finally freezing my blood.

But I wasn't going to shatter.

Clenching my fists, I lifted my head high and narrowed my eyes. "You can't have them. They belong to me now."

He laughed. "As if a mere human could stop me." He approached them. "I'll be taking those wolves now."

On top of a marble coffin with a gold crown medallion carved into the side sat a wooden box.

He followed my gaze. "Ah. Yes. That's the Rose Box. You can have it once I have my wolves." He pulled out a slender ebon rod. "This is a hellish wand. One touch and the wolves' souls will turn black and they will belong to me forever."

"*Move*," I yelled.

Bella and Luna lunged to the right, and Remus and Nico to the left.

"You can't escape," Balthazar smirked. "You're trapped here until I release you. Your friends outside can't help you, not even the reapers."

He raced over toward Bella, who was snarling in the corner, her ears flattened against her head. "You'll be mine again soon, my pretty."

I had to get the Rose Box. I bolted toward it, but I slammed into an invisible wall and flew onto my back. The fall knocked the air out of me.

"I told you, foolish girl—you can't have the Rose Box until I get my wolves back."

I scrambled to my feet. "Why do you want them so badly?"

He inched toward Bella, who was still cowering and snarling in the corner. "They're excellent trackers, especially in hunting down souls—"

"Souls that don't belong to you." A male voice interrupted.

I whirled around and my heart leapt.

The Archangel Michael stepped around the coffin. His dark hair was pulled back into a queue and he was brandishing his sword Excalibur.

"How did you get in here?" Balthazar hissed. "I warded it."

"Not good enough," Michael sneered. "Now, Balthazar, I thought I told you… these wolves don't belong to you."

Balthazar lunged toward Bella, but the wand flew from his hand and fell at Michael's feet.

Balthazar spun around, his face blazing with fury. "Damn you."

Michael narrowed his eyes and slowly headed toward him. "I'm sorry. What. Did. You. Say?"

Balthazar immediately vanished.

"Such a coward." Michael returned his sword to its sheath.

"Thank—" But just like Balthazar, he disappeared.

I thought about what I had just heard. So the archangels and Balthazar were battling over souls. That was some creepy war.

I went to get the Rose Box, but it was still behind an invisible barricade.

I rubbed my sweating forehead, desperate to get out of here before Balthazar returned. Shit, what was I going to do?

Luna nudged me.

I stroked her head. "Any ideas, girl?"

It's an Unseelie spell. You can break it, the voice from the Book of Goody urged.

Use the *Morphello Refulsi* spell? Crap, it would drain me, but what choice did I have?

I looked at my wolves. "Protect me, please."

Nico looked at me adoringly, as if to say they would do so with their lives.

I lifted a shaking arm and in a loud, clear voice, I said, *"Morphello Refulsi."*

Sensations whisked through me and pink swirls tingled around my fingers, then swooshed over toward the grave and snaked over the wall.

Something was fighting me, making my arm tremble more. My legs wobbled, and I fell onto my knees. Something wet dripped down my nose.

SHRASHH SHRASHH SHRASHH

What sounded like glass crashed to the floor. Panting hard, I dropped my arm.

My wolves nuzzled around me. "Hey, babies." I wiped my nose with my sleeve, smearing blood onto my sleeve.

I took a deep breath and forced myself to stand. "Here goes nothing." I looked down at them. "Stay here."

Nico growled.

I snapped my fingers and pointed at the ground. "I mean it."

Nico held my gaze as if challenging me, but then Remus, Luna, and Bella blocked him from following me.

I staggered toward the marble coffin. Thankfully, the force field was gone, but there could be other booby traps. Who knew what Balthazar had planted?

My body was shaking but I couldn't stop now. I reached out for the Rose Box. It felt warm in my hands. I slumped down on the cold marble floor. I tried to open the box, but the lid wouldn't budge.

Then I remembered. Blood opened the box. My blood.

"Nico, come."

The dominant wolf walked past his siblings and stood in front of me. I took off my glove and held out my hand.

"Bite," I panted.

He looked at me hesitantly.

The other wolves moved out around me.

"Nico, you have to do this. Please."

Suddenly, Luna snapped her jaws and bit down hard on my hand, drawing blood.

I cried out, and she immediately released me.

I ignored the pulsing pain. "Good girl," I whispered.

Blood dripped down the center of my palm, and I wiped it onto the Rose Box. Slowly, the lid creaked opened.

I held my breath.

25

White light streamed out of the box and poured down first my throat and then down the throat of each of my wolves. We shook uncontrollably. Power surged through me like a tidal wave, sending adrenaline pumping through me faster and faster. Any fear disappeared. I was no longer afraid to face my uncle.

I glanced at my beautiful wolves, and their eyes had changed from red to white.

More bright swirls whooshed out of the box and slid away under the door. I wasn't sure where they were going, but wherever it was, it wouldn't be good for my uncle.

I closed the box and stood. "Time to face the music."

Serenity fell over me as I headed toward the door. More troops had arrived, perhaps from Ashton's father, and their cries and screams filled my ears as battle waged on in front of me, but I ignored them. I wasn't going there. I was going to the arena.

An eagle circled overhead. It was Freedom. An enormous black bat was here too—Anton.

As if in a trance, I headed out of the cemetery.

"Salem," someone screamed.

It was Mateo. His hair was tousled and his shirt was covered in blood, but I instinctively knew it wasn't his. For now, he was okay.

I spotted Faas and Ari on the battlefield. Faas was throwing fireballs, burning wolves and soldiers alive. Ari fought with a sword.

A spell popped into my mind unbidden and I placed the Rose Box down in front of my boots. I spread my arms wide. *"Imperiseo Vilasi."*

Once again, pink swirls shot out of my fingertips and whizzed all around the fighting warriors and wolves, causing complete pandemonium.

"Ah!" Men cried out and dropped their weapons.

Wolves shifted back into humans.

"What the hell?" Faas shook his hand. "I can't make any fireballs."

Then Stefan, Rusty, and Julie popped onto the field.

Stefan looked the two Dark Demons up and down. "Time to go back to the Hollows, boys."

"Never." Faas turned to run, but Julie touched his shoulder with her scythe. The two vanished.

Ari took off at top speed, but Rusty flashed in front of him.

"Going somewhere, asshole?"

Ari changed direction but ran right into Stefan, who touched him with his scythe. All three of them disappeared into thin air.

"What's happening?" A bewildered soldier asked.

I wasn't sure, but I knew it had something to do with the Rose Box and my new power.

Gloria rushed over to me, shivering. She was naked and must have been fighting as her wolf. "Salem, your eyes...the wolves..."

I looked at her and smiled. "It is time. The final battle is between me and my uncle. Winner takes all."

Tears welled in Gloria's eyes as Mateo joined us. "But you

don't understand. It's Ashton. Velkan attacked him with some kind of spear. He's…"

Gunnar ran up, panting. "He's not dead, but I've never felt the dark magic that's coming off him before. I can't…I can't heal him. I don't know why."

Gloria held her arms. "The guard Edward, I think his name was, guarded Ashton's body. He even fought Velkan."

I frowned. "What happened?"

"He slashed his sword at Edward, but Rusty showed up. Velkan left."

"Edward's not waking up either," Gunnar said glumly.

Mateo ran his hand through his tangled hair. "Salem, this is too dangerous. You don't know what could happen in the arena."

I looked at him sorrowfully. "You can't stop this. Nobody can. This is my destiny."

Everyone was staring at me and my wolves. This was it. This was the moment I had been waiting for—to confront the man who murdered my parents, who tortured my mate and my friends, and who stole my crown.

"Please pick up the Rose Box." I turned slowly away from Mateo. "It is time to go." My voice had a new, regal tone to it that even I didn't recognize.

I could hear footsteps behind me as I headed for the arena. Mateo, my friends, and the armies were all following me. I had never been to the arena, didn't even know the way, but something drew me there. It was located just south of Moon Kingdom and west of the Moonlight Gardens Cemetery and at last it came into view, all white marble and looking like the coliseum in ancient Rome, but not decaying. It was pristine.

The entrance gates stood open, and I knew my uncle was waiting for me on the field. This was it. I should be trembling in my boots and running for the hills, but I was still blanketed in the same strange sense of calm.

I followed a corridor that went down onto the snow-covered

field. My uncle Calvin stood there, completely naked. He was thinner than in the pictures I had seen of him and he had a look in his eyes that would have curdled milk. A brittle smile spread across his hawkish face.

He flashed an appraising gaze over me. “So, you actually made it. I didn’t think you were going to come.”

I narrowed my eyes. “Thanks to you, I almost didn’t.”

He chuckled. “You didn’t think it would be a breeze to get here, did you?” The smugness in his voice made me want to slap the matching smile right off his face.

He snapped his fingers, and Velkan appeared.

“Balthazar has a message for you. He says you have to pay.” Velkan had the same black wand in his hand that Balthazar had in the mausoleum. He twirled it thoughtfully in his fingers. “I already got your friend with this. Now it’s your turn.”

He lifted his arm, ready to stab me with it.

I held out my palm and the pinks swirls swished around him. Velkan screamed in agony and disappeared.

Calvin’s eyes widened. “What the hell?”

I glared. “I don’t like dark magic, and once again, you’re cheating.”

He shrugged. “You say that like it’s a bad thing. I like to win. I’ve brought your friends. Come, say hello.”

Behind him, guards held my Aunt Remi’s thin arms. She looked like she could barely stand. Her red hair hung in front of her face, looking more skeletal than human. My friend Quint wasn’t faring much better. He had a thick chain around his neck that I assumed blocked his vampire powers. His arms were bound behind his back, and his ankles were shackled.

“Let them go,” I said. “This battle doesn’t have anything to do with them.”

“No. You have my wo—” He frowned. “What happened to their eyes?”

I gave him a tight smile. “I opened the Rose Box.”

He gritted his teeth. "Give it to me."

"You can have it if you defeat me. How's that?"

He moistened his lips and beads of sweat slid down his face. People were filing into the coliseum, getting ready to watch us.

"I think—"

A huge bat glided into the arena and then shifted into Anton. He gave Calvin a long, hard stare. "You will engage in a fair fight, King Calvin."

Calvin stretched out his arms in appeal. "She was to come alone."

Anton looked at him curiously. "She is alone."

"The demon wolves are with her."

"Ah, but you claim they are yours, don't you?"

Calvin clamped his jaw shut tight.

"And we are merely here to witness this match." Anton took a letter out of his pocket. "Those were your very words and we will hold you to them."

Freedom landed on one side of Anton, and Hayley flashed on the other. She looked beautiful. Her hair and face were clean, and she had on a long black woolen coat, yoga pants, and boots.

The blood drained from Calvin's face, and he frowned. "I don't understand. You're…you're supposed to be locked up."

She gave him a wide grin. "The Rose Box has been opened, remember?"

"How can that be? She doesn't have the key."

Hayley laughed softly. "She herself was the key. Her blood."

"You bitch," he growled.

Hayley scowled. "A word of warning, *Master*: you no longer control me and you will have to fight Salem fair and square."

I cast my gaze over him in disgust. "So, that's how you won all your fights in the arena before—black magic?"

Hayley lowered her head. "Something I truly regret."

"That is something you are not responsible for." Anton put his hand on her shoulder. "You were enslaved."

Anton stepped away from us and spread out his arms. "Listen to me, all of you. It is the Winter Solstice and the day of the battle for the crown of the Moon Kingdom is here. This is a fight to the death, as per King Calvin's own orders."

Calvin ran his long fingers through his hair and looked uneasy. "Those wolves can't be here."

I slowly undressed, never taking my eyes off him. He could whine all he wanted. My wolves weren't going anywhere.

Anton tilted his head. "Hayley, please return to your seat and take Salem's clothes with you."

She quickly picked up my clothes, but then hesitated before she left, giving me an uneasy look and silently mouthing, 'Good luck.'

I nodded, barely acknowledging her. My focus was squarely on Calvin, who was getting desperate and clearly would like nothing better than to rip out my lungs.

Anton clapped his hands. "Let the fight begin."

My uncle shifted first, and my eyes widened. Oh, shit. He was huge, bigger than I thought he would be. He was almost as big as my wolf, and I was enormous.

I shifted and my demon wolves disappeared one by one. I couldn't see them, but I could *feel* them. They were part of me. They were inside me. Their power pumped through me.

My uncle lunged, his jaws aiming for my throat. I barely got out of the way in time. Shit, this dude was serious. I snarled and bared my teeth.

"You bastard, Calvin."

"Bitch."

"Cheater."

"Let's hear it for the king."

I couldn't separate all the various boos, hisses, and cheers coming from the crowded arena, and right now, I didn't care.

Calvin and I circled each other, sizing each other up.

He instigated another attack, but this time, I was ready for him. I escaped his jaw and bit his ear, nearly ripping it off.

"Salem, Salem, Salem!"

"Boo. She's not our queen and never will be. Cal-vin. Cal-vin."

The encouragement mixed with the taunts rocked the stadium.

Calvin yelped and jerked away, his ear dangling. The metallic taste of blood rolled around in my mouth.

Calvin charged, and I met him head on. He bit my neck, tearing into my flesh, the agony momentarily weakening me. He pushed me onto the ground, his paws ripping into my flesh. Fear nearly crippled me. The bastard weighed a ton, and I didn't know if I could buck him off me. Even as the pain pounded through me, something else was happening inside me. Power pulsed through me, making my determination even stronger.

With one big shove, I got him off me. Blood drenched my fur, and I panted. He circled me, waiting to seize the next opportunity to kill me.

He lunged, but I was ready. We smashed into each other, biting and clawing. Blood and fur were flying. Pain and anguish blinded me to everything, but I needed it to stop. Flashing memories of everything this man had done exploded inside me and I smashed my teeth into his neck and tossed him into the air. He dropped back onto the ground and I was on him in a second, pinning his shoulders. Then I bent my head down, and in one swift motion, ripped out his throat.

He whimpered and then went silent.

It was over.

It was finally over.

I spat out his foul flesh and then collapsed as I shifted back. Everything hurt and I felt like I was choking on my own blood. My wolves flashed before me. Blood streaked their fur, and they were panting. As I fluttered in and out of consciousness, I thought of Mateo.

"Queen, queen, queen."

"Salem, Salem."

Someone gathered me into their arms. Mateo looked down at me, his face crumbling. "Oh, God. Salem, no. Don't leave me."

Was I dying? I stared into his beautiful brown eyes. The stupid fear I had of not telling him how I felt seemed so pointless now. I couldn't leave without saying it.

I cupped his cheek and was surprised to see blood streaking down my hand. He clasped it and kissed my palm.

"Mateo…I…love you." My voice was so weak that I wasn't sure he heard me.

Tears glistened in his eyes. "Salem. No, no. Stay with me."

I wanted to obey him, but my eyes closed and I couldn't open them. Then I remembered no more.

My eyes fluttered open, and I realized I was in a fancy bedroom. Canopy bed…ornate furniture…shit, I knew this room—it was Calvin's bedchamber.

"You're finally awake."

I jerked my head and instantly decided that hadn't been a smart thing to do. "Mateo?"

He sat on my bed. "You're alive."

"Gunnar healed me?"

"Yeah, that guy has the mojo all right. There were many he had to heal."

I scanned the room. "My wolves?"

"See for yourself."

As if on cue, one head after another popped up and rested on my bed. "They're okay?"

"They're fine." He kissed my shaking hand.

"And the others? My aunt and Quint?"

"They're fine too." There was something in his voice.

Tears slid down my cheeks. "And Ashton?" My voice cracked.

"He's not dead, but neither Hades nor Gunnar can heal him. We don't know why. Anton's researching it."

I patted my bed. "Okay, but why am I in this creepy bed?"

"This is the monarch's bedroom. You're the new queen."

"Yes, but it's his bed. I don't want to be here."

"You don't have a choice. All the other rooms are full."

I frowned. "With the wounded?"

He lay down next to me. "No, because of your coronation. The guests have started arriving already."

My eyes widened. "What?"

He pushed my hair back. "Salem, you won. Anton and Hayley showed the other kings the proof in the Rose Box that your uncle murdered your parents and that you were the rightful heir. They have accepted you wholeheartedly."

This was all happening so fast. "Will you just hold me?"

He wrapped his arms around me and we lay in silence as I listened to his heartbeat that was music to my ears.

"So, I'm going to be queen, huh?"

He kissed the top of my head. "Yes, you are. You're everything everyone's hoped for."

I looked up at him and grinned. "Well then, I have just one question."

He rubbed my back. "What?"

He was so handsome and had always believed in me, even when I hadn't. He'd been there when I needed him the most. "Mateo, will you marry me?"

"With all the royalty available to you, I'm not sure they'd accept me. I'm just a royal guard, Salem."

I straddled his hips, feeling his hard flesh, and his eyes widened.

He clasped my thighs. "Salem, what are you doing? You just woke up and you're not completely healed."

I put my hands on his chest. "Do you remember the cave?"

"How could I forget?"

"You healed me then, after Faas burned me."

He scoffed as he ran his hands up and down my arms. "No, Gunnar did that."

"Mostly, but you're my mate and you healed the rest of me and you know it."

I unzipped his jeans.

He clasped my hands. "Salem—"

"I want you to heal me and I want you to marry me. The people will accept you eventually." I broke free of his grasp and put my hands on his broad shoulders. "You're everything I've ever hoped for. I love you, you stubborn wolf. You're mine."

He cocked his eyebrow. "So, you really do love me?"

"With every fiber of my being."

He smiled like he'd just gotten the last piece of cheesecake. "Do you know how long I've waited for you to say those words? You were practically dying before you uttered them, and I wasn't sure if you even remembered."

"I've always loved you. It's just that growing up the way I did, trust never came easy, but I seriously can't do this whole queen thing without you. I need you."

A mischievous glint twinkled in his eye. "So, you really want me to heal you?"

I balled my fists in his shirt. "Yes. And I want you to rule by my side."

I held my breath, not sure what his answer would be.

He gently rolled me onto my back. "With a proposition like that, how could I say no?"

I smiled like a lovesick fool. "So, you'll marry me?"

"I always thought I'd be the one asking, but yes."

"Then seal it with a kiss, my king."

His lips captured mine, kissing me with a thoroughness that stripped my mind of everything but him. His tongue explored my mouth, probing deep, penetrating the last of my defenses, tearing them down forever.

And he kept his promise, healing me over and over that night until I fell into a blissful sleep, listening to his heartbeat.

Did you love this series? This is the end of Salem's and Mateo's story. However, did you want to learn more about Ebony's and Gunnar's story?

Would like a free book? Get Legacy Academy: The Early Years!

If you want to find out about Ebony and Gunnar, you'll want to dive into Legacy Academy first and learn about Ebony's sister Raven. Become a Legacy! Grab Legacy Academy!

Welcome to Legacy Academy!

There are three rules at this supernatural academy:

1—Date your own kind. Mixing with other races is forbidden.

2—Never speak or look at The Royals, the powerful princes destined to rule each of their kingdoms.

3—Avoid the human world.

Of course, I've already broken all the rules.

There's something different about me.

Something that's not pure.

I'm not like the other dragon shifters. Maybe it's because of my human blood.

The Royals have noticed me, and every girl at the Academy hates me.

I never knew the paranormal world existed until one day I have a fight with Mom, I come home to find her gone, and poof, I'm a dragon shifter.

It would have been nice if Mom would have told me. But then again, secrets rule my family…

But now she's been kidnapped and I have no answers. I have to find her. Some powerful demon is after me, because supposedly I'm a threat to his power. Which is crazy! Has he seen me in class?

Grab this new romance academy and enroll in Legacy where you'll meet dragons, wolves, demons, Fae, and vampires!

You can even get a free book if you sign up for my newsletter!

DEAR READER

I wanted to thank you for taking a chance on me. This is the final book in the Wolf Princess trilogy, and I hope you enjoyed it. I'm almost sad to see that it's done because I loved Salem and Mateo.

The trilogy is finished, but I have decided to a story about Ashton and Gloria. Yes, you will find out what needs to happen with their story. I just wanted Ashton and Gloria to have a happily ever after in Wolf Protector.

If you like this book, I have other books in this world where you can learn about Ebony's and Gunnar's story.

If you never want to miss a new release from me, then sign up for my newsletter and become a Legacy! You'll get the first book in the series that it stared it all—Legacy Academy: The Early Years!!

I also have a private Facebook if you would like to come and play with me. I have giveaways and we just have fun. This is another way for you to become a Legacy!

I hope I'll see you around!

M Guida

ABOUT THE AUTHOR

M Guida has always loved fantasy and romance, especially dragons. Growing up, she devoured fantasy books and all kinds of young adult books. And then she found romance and a whole new world opened up to her.

Now as an adult, she fell in love with academy romance and has blended all of her past loves into one compelling series. Dragons, vampires, elves, demons, and shifters all attend Legacy Academy.

When she's not writing, she lives in the colorful Rocky Mountains with her fur baby, Raven, and enjoys taking her for walks.

If you never want to miss a new release, sign up for her newsletter and get Legacy Academy The Early Years for free!

ALSO BY M GUIDA

Wolf Princess:

Wolf Princess

Wolf Prince

Wolf Mate

Academy for Reapers:

Academy for Reapers Year One

Academy for Reapers Year Two

Academy for Reapers Year Three

Academy for Reapers Year Four

Legacy Series:

Before Legacy: The Early Years

Legacy Year One

Legacy Year Two

Legacy Year Three

Legacy Year Four

Ebony's Legacy Year One

Ebony's Legacy Year Two

Ebony's Legacy Year Three

Ebony's Legacy Year Four

Collections:

Legacy Academy Collection One

Before Legacy Series:

Before Legacy: Armond

Before Legacy: Gunnar

The Defenders

Wolf Defender

Vella Story:

Bite Me: Vampire's Forbidden Romance

Made in the USA
Thornton, CO
04/23/23 21:01:57

2877c1a6-3484-48a5-9abc-c607dfba2a2aR01